I0607872

Play Action Pass

Gina Ardito

Published by Gina Ardito, 2020.

PLAY ACTION PASS

First edition. September 16, 2020.

Written by Gina Ardito.

DEDICATION

For all the parents who've sat on the field in blazing heat, driving rain, and blustery temperatures to cheer on your personal sports legend.

Chapter 1

"**Y**ou've *got* to be kidding me."

Jordan Fawcett stared at his boss standing a few feet from the other side of his desk and silently willed her to break into a grin that would let him in on the joke.

Susan Harwich didn't flinch. She kept her expression solemn, folded her arms over her chest, and replied, "I'm afraid not. The selling agent's adamant. According to the Loughlin Building's current owner, right of first refusal for the place has to go to the Delgado Foundation. Rumor has it they're looking for a new site for their downtown school, and I guess someone on the board over there thinks their property might be perfect. The good news is, if we get Cameron Delgado to bite, they'll pay us double our standard commission. If not, we still get the listing. But we can't entertain any other offers or even show it to anyone else until Delgado turns it down. And I want you to convince her to buy it. Not pass, not think about it. Sign-on-the-dotted-line-buy-it."

He studied the glossy photo paperclipped to the top of the manila folder, and his stomach fumbled. "You know I wanted to lease that space."

"Yes, but Delgado can afford to buy it outright. Susan's Rule Number One in the corporate real estate business: A sale from a wealthy, established client is always better than a lease offer from a brand new business venture with no track record. No offense."

"None taken." Only because he didn't have a choice.

Jordan ran a finger over the image of the two-story red brick façade, which contained decoratively arched windows framed by stacked bricks duplicating that same shape into the building itself in three-dimension. Very late nineteenth century architecture, he surmised, with a gothic flair. Fancy and old-world charming at the same time.

A narrow alley on the right, covered by a red-and-black striped awning, led to a leafy courtyard in the rear. On the cover of the folder, details written in fine point marker, a Susan habit, listed such perks as eleven-thousand-square-feet of interior space; tall ceilings with exposures on the north, south, and west; two dozen available parking spaces; and a corner location. Not that he needed the details. He'd practically memorized them from the moment the listing came into the office.

He could see Cam wanting this site, if she was, indeed, on the lookout for a new property. It had the right look, the right location, the right feel to it. Which were all the reasons *he'd* wanted it for him and Marcus.

"*Double* commission, Jordan," Susan prompted when he didn't speak again.

The asking price was mid-seven figures. Normally, for double commission, he'd sell an igloo to the devil. But there wasn't enough money in the world to get him involved with Cameron Delgado again. His days of reaching for the stars were long gone. Now, all he wanted was the rehab center he and Marcus planned to open. If he wasn't going to get the building they wanted for their first location, he could live with that. But he couldn't stand by and watch—no, *help*—Cam swoop in to steal it out from under him—all because she had the business-slash-financial clout and connections he didn't have the good fortune to be born with.

He picked up the folder and thrust it toward Susan. "I've already got a full roster with the condos down by Hudson Yards. Tell Michaela to handle this. Or you do it. Use that old 'It's tough to be a woman in a man's field' shtick you played on Tanya Lowell two months ago." No way in hell Cam would fall for it, but that could only work in his favor.

"Oh, for God's sake," Susan retorted with an exaggerated eye roll. "Susan's Rule Number Two: never use the same shtick twice."

"Then try another."

"I plan to," she said with a smirk. "That's why I'm assigning this sale to *you*."

He shook his head and waved the folder to get her to take it. She didn't budge. With an air of defeat, he sighed. "Don't ask me to do this, Susan."

"I'm sorry, but you're our best shot. No one here knows her like you do. You dated her. You played on her father's old football team. Either one of those facts on its own would make you perfect to handle this deal. Having *both* on your resume means you're the one person working here who has insight into Duke Delgado's daughter and the foundation—an 'in' the rest of us will never have. Therefore, you're the one who's going to make this happen."

Picking up his staple remover, he gave her a caustic laugh. "Now I *know* you're kidding. I dated Cameron years ago, and we didn't exactly part on the best of terms." While he listed off his reasons not to get involved with this deal, he squeezed the remover between his fingers like a stress ball. "As for the football team, I allowed myself to be traded off the Vanguard, and she saw my move as the ultimate betrayal. After that happened, I was dead to her—literally. Hell, she didn't even bother to send a note when I broke my back. A total stranger would have a better 'in' than I would."

"Then you'll have to apologize to soften her up." She wagged a finger. "And don't even think about sabotaging this deal so you can lease the site for yourself. If I hear one whisper that you didn't give this opportunity a hundred and ten percent, I'll not only refuse to give you second-shot, I'll also blacklist you with every reputable realtor in the city."

The squeezing grew more frenetic, the squeal of the hinge the only sound in the room. "You actually think I'm going to humble myself so she can have..."

Susan planted a fist on his desk and leaned closer until they were practically nose-to-nose. "Be very careful what you say next, Jordan. This is a multi-million dollar deal. The firm could use this sale, as well as any future sales that come because of it. Another building will come along for your little venture. But a deal with the Delgado Foundation comes along once in a lifetime. Now, you can either take on this property and I'll transfer the Hudson Yards condos to Michaela, or you can find another place to work and Michaela will get *all* your listings. Your choice."

He dropped the packet of property information onto his desk and tossed the staple remover atop the manila folder. A deep exhale escaped his pursed lips.

Apparently, Susan took the sound as a victory for her. With a smug grin, she turned on her chunky heels and strode away, only pausing long enough to toss over her shoulder, "Try flowers. Most women *love* roses. If things between you two are as bad as you say, I'd suggest hundreds of them."

He glared at her retreating back, visually flinging imaginary knives between her shoulder blades. *Ha-ha.*

Once she'd left his office, he scrubbed his hands over his face. Why? He'd been back in New York for two years now and had managed to avoid everything connected to his past here. Since his return, he hadn't visited any of the old haunts: the restaurants, parks, stores, or even the stadium they'd once hung out at together. He'd built a whole new life with a new job, new friends, and new plans. He didn't want to see Cam again—not yet. Not until he'd changed his world so much that he no longer remembered how she used to make him feel, and how, in the end, it had all been a lie.

A few deep breathing exercises cooled his rising temper, and he tried to look at the situation with a clearer head. Six figures would be a nice addition to his bottom line. Marcus would be pissed, but if he explained that in the long run, they'd be able to look for another site and have more money to spend on equipment, or a bigger place, or just a fatter cushion to help them get through the lean years until the business took off—which they both knew would happen—maybe this could work to their benefit. There weren't many physical therapies in New York that could accommodate all kinds of disabilities for athletes and professionals. Theirs would. So okay, they'd probably lose the Loughlin property. In the long run, though, they might be better off.

Plus, there was a delicious irony in using Cameron Delgado's money to fund a future that wouldn't include her. And maybe...

He turned to his keyboard and typed in the Delgado Foundation's website. Maybe he could handle this sale without ever having anything to do with Cam. After all, as the president, she probably didn't have many dealings with the day-to-day operations. He clicked on "Meet Our Board of Directors" and began his search there. Who among these unfamiliar names would most likely be involved in the acquisition of their new site? Treasurer?

Well, why not start with the money guy? If Martin K. Jacobs wasn't actually handling the deal, he could probably direct Jordan to the right contact. Cam would never have to know.

Picking up his receiver, he dialed the number and waited for someone to answer. When the receptionist went into her spiel, he let her finish then asked to speak to Mr. Jacobs.

"Whom may I say is calling?"

"I'm Jordan Fawcett with HRR Commercial Realtors. We have a property coming up for sale I think might be perfect for the foundation's new site here in New York and I'd like to give the foundation first look."

"Mr. Jacobs isn't in charge of that transaction. Hold on please, and I'll transfer you to Ms. Delgado."

"No, wait—"

Too late. He was placed on hold while his call was sent directly to the one person he dreaded talking to. Dammit! Now, what? He didn't dare hang up. For one thing, Susan would have his desk cleaned out before he could utter a word of explanation. For another, the possibility Cam would find out and think he'd chickened out dented his already-too-battered pride where she was concerned. He'd needed her once before and she'd turned her back. He couldn't let her turn her back on him again. This time, he'd make her face him.

Another deep breath. Okay, fine. He'd handle this acquisition the way he would any other: with efficiency and professionalism. This was a business deal, not a marriage proposal. Simply because she'd rejected the latter didn't mean history would repeat itself on the former.

The piped-in music changed to a single jangle, and a sunny voice answered, "Ms. Delgado's office, this is Val."

Val. He remembered her—slightly. Petite, blond, an eager go-getter Cam had hired about six months before their breakup. Nice to see she still retained some loyalty for her staff.

"Good morning, Val," he greeted with false enthusiasm. "My name is Jordan Fawcett. I'm with HRR Corporate Realty. I'd like to speak to Ms. Delgado regarding a property we have available we think may be a perfect fit for the foundation's current *and future* needs."

"Great pitch. Nice touch, adding in the future bit," the woman replied, a smile evident in her tone. "Unfortunately, Ms. Delgado is unavailable for the next several days. However, I'm compiling an inventory of possible sites for her review. Why don't you tell me what you've got? If it meets our requirements, I'll be happy to add your property to the list."

It couldn't be that easy. His spine tingled. "What happens after that? I mean, when can I expect to hear from you should my site be the one that suits your needs?"

"Ms. Delgado will make the final determination. We want to move forward on this quickly, so I would expect she'll be scheduling appointments within the next week or two. Let me just ask you a few questions, and I can let you know right now if I'll be passing your property on to her, okay?"

"Okay."

For the next several minutes, he answered the woman's questions regarding location, square footage, available parking, and a dozen other particulars, thanks mostly to the notes Susan had written in her fine tip marker. The H of HRR Corporate Realty had done her homework, which explained how she managed to stay at the top of the New York corporate real estate game, year after year.

"Congratulations, Mr. Fawcett," Val said at last. "Your property makes the cut. We'll be in touch for more information as things develop. Thanks for contacting us."

They each said goodbye, and Jordan hung up, then tilted his head toward the ceiling. Despite the promise of his discussion with Val, a sense of dread settled on his shoulders. He was attempting to put his future in Cam Delgado's hands. Again.

He'd tried to be part of her world once before, only to have his heart ripped out of his chest and stuck on a pike before she kicked him out and slammed the door in his face. What would she take from him this time?

What was left? Hell, he had nothing. Not his dream career, not the woman he'd thought loved him, not even the use of his legs.

"Life," he said aloud to the empty room, "sucks."

CAMERON DELGADO STOOD outside the third building on their list, and a shiver of delight danced across her bare arms. The ground floor windows would let in lots of natural light, and the courtyard in the back could easily be converted into a small playground. *If the interior looks half as good as the exterior, we could have a winner here.* "Parking?" she asked.

Her assistant, Valerie Sullivan, checked her notes. "Twenty-three slots on the side. Two handicapped, but I think we could create at least three more with a quick redesign. It already has ramp access, and the rear doors are within width guidelines. According to the agent, this place was last used as the main office for a marine insurance company. What do you think marine insurance is for? Like, do they pay out if someone falls overboard on your boat?"

Cam snorted a laugh. "No. They insure cargo and ships and other transport used in the transfer of the cargo."

"Well, whatever they used to do, Three Sails Marine has closed up shop. This place looks pretty good, if I do say so myself." She flipped to the second page of her notes. "Eight offices upstairs, plus two restrooms. First floor is a large open workspace with four restrooms and a kitchen in the back. Not a cafeteria, more a small breakroom with a bank of cabinets, a fridge, microwave shelf, and one of those industrial coffeemakers that serves free sludge all day to keep the employees from going outside and running away screaming."

This time, Cam burst into full-blown laughter. "And you would know that because...?"

"I used to work in a similar place. Before I came to the foundation. You live and die by the amount of paperwork you push out each day or how many clicks you make on your computer. It's depressing, demoralizing, and draining." She looked up at the building and flipped up her middle finger. "Good riddance to Three Sails Marine Insurance. Hello to us or any other company that can fill this place with joy and laughter."

"A-men."

Funny. She and Val worked so well together, it was hard for Cam to remember a time she didn't have this capable, hardworking woman beside her, backing her up and keeping on top of all the minor crises that developed day after day, year after year.

She made a mental note to check Val's current salary. It might be time to give her a raise. Cam valued her too much to lose her. Now, especially with this latest challenge: finding a new location for their Manhattan youth center. Her mind zipping through a dozen different topics at once, Cam strode around the corner, drinking in the colorful awnings and signs for the nearby shops, the proximity of the subway station, and the steady groups of pedestrians taking advantage of a beautiful spring day. Nice building, great location, She'd set aside the entire day to do a rudimentary inspection of the top ten sites on Val's list. And here at barely nine-thirty in the morning, she might have already found the winner. Yes, Val was a real gem.

"Eleven thousand square feet, you said?"

Her assistant followed close behind. "That's what the agent told me."

She studied the old bricks and the cornerstone etched with a date of 1898. Any commercial buildings built prior to 1960 were approximately twelve thousand square feet, so this one was right in the ballpark.

"Put this site on the shortlist. I'll contact the agent this afternoon. I'm going to want to see the inside."

Val pulled the pen from behind her ear and circled the address on her sheaf of papers. "You got it."

"Do we have a copy of the current floor plan?"

"The agent was supposed to fax it over today."

"Well, if we don't have it by the time we get back to the office, I'll request it again when I make the appointment to go over the interior."

Cam took one more quick walk-around while snapping pictures of the site from all different angles before heading toward the black car parked at the curb. "Where to next?"

"Hell's Kitchen," Val replied as she shuffled the stapled papers in her hand. "Ninth Avenue."

"Great. Let's go. You've done a terrific job vetting these, Val. I'm really impressed. Thank you."

Val beamed. "No sweat. I mean, this one came to me via Ashlynn in Mr. Jacobs's office. Apparently, the agent heard about our search through the real estate grapevine and contacted us directly with what he thought might be a perfect fit."

"He might not have been wrong," Cam murmured. As she climbed into the back seat, she stole another look at the building that had already captured her imagination before sliding over for Val to join her. Interesting. "Do we know if anyone else is looking at the property?"

"I was assured we were getting first crack."

Once they were inside the cool interior and Val had provided their driver with the next address, Cam held out a hand. "Let me see the write-up for this space."

"Sure." Val passed over the packet of stapled papers, folded to page two where a spreadsheet of neat columns listed all the building's pertinent details, including specs, remaining furnishings, utilities, and other particulars Val thought Cam should know.

Cam settled against the black leather seat and ran an index finger across each column, as if she could absorb the figures through her skin and then be able to recall them with a snap. Everything she read only made her more certain that this particular property was the ideal locale for the new youth center.

Out on the street, a car horn blared in an ear-splitting soliloquy, followed by the squeal of brakes, and as their driver stopped short to avoid colliding with the car in front of them, both Cam and Val shot forward with the momentum. The packets of papers dropped to the floor in a scattered heap.

"Goddammit, what the hell are you doing?" the driver shouted before catching hold of his temper. Using the rearview mirror, he looked at his passengers. "Sorry, Ms. Delgado. Ms. Sullivan. You ladies okay?"

Cam slipped back into position and smoothed her skirt while Val gathered up the notes on the various properties. "We're fine, Ted. Just a little shaken up. What happened?"

"Not a hundred percent sure. I'm guessing a driver up in front stopped short when the light changed, but it caused a chain reaction at least five cars long. You sure you're all right?"

Cam glanced at Val, who nodded. "We're fine," she repeated as Val handed her the packet she'd been reading before the minor excitement. "Thanks."

While Val shuffled through the rest, Cam returned her attention to the details on the building they'd just left. Two lines in, she realized something was off. On a hunch, she flipped to the first page to note the address on top. "This is the wrong prospectus."

Val leaned toward her to confirm the error. "Oops. Sorry. That's where we're headed." She took the packet back and flipped through the remaining stapled paperwork. "Here you go."

With a smile, Cam took the offered pages. But the smile froze on her face when she noted the name of the agent written at the top of page one: Jordan Fawcett.

It couldn't be. Her heart thudded inside her rib cage, and her mouth went dry. A roar rose between her ears, drowning out all sound.

"Cam?" Val's voice seemed to come from some deep tunnel. "You okay? Cam?"

She managed a nod, but speech deserted her, and her mind stayed mired in thoughts of the name on the page. Jordan Fawcett. It couldn't be. Oh, sure. She knew he'd come back to New York after his football career was shattered due to an injury during a game. But he'd *killed* their relationship long before then.

Why, all of a sudden, did he get in touch with her? To sell her a building? After all the crap he'd put her through, he could come up with the Taj Mahal of buildings and she'd refuse to do business with him.

Tossing the packet of papers at Val, she found enough voice to announce, "On second thought, this place won't work. What else have we got?"

Val flashed a confused expression for the briefest of moments, then smoothed her face into her usual confident business mien. "Hell's Kitchen's next. We'll go from there."

Cam turned to stare out the window. "Good."

If Jordan Fawcett thought he could just waltz back into her life, he'd underestimated her ability to hold a grudge. Like her mother, she could nurse her grievances for a lifetime. And in Jordan's case, even longer.

Chapter 2

"That agent called. The one for the Loughlin site? I told him you're reviewing other properties."

Cam sat with her back to her desk, staring out the windows at the river and the rest of the city skyline. She wished her assistant had told him to take a hike instead. Although, she winced at her own callousness, maybe not in those *specific* terms.

"Your coffee's getting cold," Val pointed out. "You want me to get you a fresh cup?"

"No, thanks." Her mind wasn't on coffee.

While physically, she was in her office, mentally, she was back outside that perfect building, staring at the intricate brickwork and the rows of windows while visualizing the property alive with the laughter and conversations of children and teens.

Why did Jordan have to be the agent representing the property? Of all the possibilities she and Val had checked out the other day, only that one made her tingle with promise. Oh, a few of the others were *okay*, but none of them pushed all her buttons the way the Loughlin Building did.

When they returned to the office after looking at the rest of the sites on Val's list, there was the faxed floor plan, as promised, waiting on her desk for her review. She needed no more than a brief perusal to conclude Jordan's property would be the easiest for her crew to rehab to fit their needs.

She sighed. Great location, great price, great building. Worst person in the world to have to deal with to get it.

God, she hated herself right now! What kind of director put her personal animosity above the needs of a charitable foundation? She'd run this organization for a decade. They trusted her to always have their best interests at heart. How could she go to the board and tell them they'd have to settle for a site that was more expensive, less accessible, and would require more time and work to fit their requirements, simply because she had a scarred history with the agent repping the more ideal site?

"Cam?" Val prompted. "You okay?"

Before she could give more than a jerky nod in response, the phone at Val's desk out in the reception area rang.

"I'm on it," Val said and rushed from her office.

Saved by the bell. Cam turned from the window and settled in her chair behind the desk. She had to focus. The New York building issue wasn't the only problem demanding her attention right now. She still had to write her speech for the Awards Dinner next week, a task she routinely put off 'til the last minute because of the tornado of emotions it engendered. Maybe she should work on it now. Maybe, if she concentrated on something besides Jordan, an answer to how to deal with the Jordan issue would organically develop. Her fingers brushed her keyboard, waking up her screensaver—a photo of a dozen children of various ages and ethnicities showing off their art projects at a festival a few years ago—when Val's voice intruded into her thoughts yet again.

"Cam? Your mother's on line one."

Well, crap. Her already dismal mood spiraled straight down into the fiery pits of hell. Much as she'd love to have Val tell Mom she was in a meeting and unreachable, Cam could never bring herself to lie to her mother—even through proxy.

On a deep inhale and a muttered, "Give me strength," she picked up the receiver and popped a finger on the blinking light.

"Good afternoon, Mother. How are you today?"

"Cameron, darling, I hope I'm not catching you at a bad time."

Every time her mother intruded was a bad time, as far as she was concerned. Nonetheless, Cam forced the lighthearted air her mother always expected from her. "Of course not. What's up?"

"Have you picked up your gown for next Friday yet?"

Ha. Next Friday. Sometimes her mother's parental intuition scared the crap out of her. The gown her mother referenced was for the same event she needed the speech for. The annual Duke Delgado Awards ceremony, complete with a five-course dinner and lots of schmoozing, was a major fundraiser for the foundation, as well as one of the sports world's biggest social events. If not for the money that poured into the foundation's coffers, thanks to the many wealthy guests in attendance, Cam would skip the pomp and circumstance for an evening at home with a pint of ice cream and a cheesy television sitcom re-run.

"I just got a call from Elaine that my dress is ready," her mother continued, "and I thought maybe we could do our final fittings together, then go to lunch afterward—my treat. We can make a day of it. I'd love to see what you plan to wear. Who knows? I might have the perfect piece of jewelry you need to finish off your look."

Cam clicked on her schedule, opened to today's agenda. "I wish I could, but my calendar is filled up solid until the night of the gala."

Not a hundred percent truthful, but she'd barely steeled her emotions for the endless hours she'd have to spend listening to her mother's disparagements on Friday night. Any additional time spent under her mother's critical eye would batter her ego to the point she'd be unable to leave her apartment for a month.

"Oh?" Even through the phone, Cam honed in on the disappointment in that one syllable uttered by Mom. "Well, did you pick up your dress already? If not, I can always swing around and grab it for you when I go to my fitting."

No way. First of all, this whole "I'll be happy to help you out" shtick was a way for Mom to get a sneak peek at Cam's dress so she could list all the reasons it was inappropriate or unflattering or too short or too long or too...whatever. Then she'd insist on dragging her daughter to *her* designer for something Cam would find too tight, too boxy, too stiff, too plain or too...whatever. Not to mention, Cam didn't want to admit she'd bought a dress off the rack at her favorite boutique a week ago. Mother would have a dozen fits over the very idea of her daughter wearing a garment a hundred other women might also wear to an entirely different event on an entirely different evening.

"My dress is already hanging in my closet at home, just waiting to be slipped into on Friday night, but thanks for offering."

"All right, then. I guess I'll have to go by myself. Do you want Andrew and me to shoot by and pick you up that night? It might be nice to arrive together as a family."

And have to stay until they were ready to leave, when they were the two people she'd prefer to avoid most? "No, thanks," she said—a bit too quickly and with too much fervor. "I mean, I appreciate the offer, but I may be coming straight from the office, so I'll just use the car service."

"You work too hard, Cameron."

"I like what I do, Mother. Don't you feel the same way about your jewelry?"

"My, yes! Why, when I'm working on a particularly intricate piece, I'd probably go days without eating if Andrew didn't remind me. That's why you need a husband, sweetheart. Someone besides me to tell you when you're working too hard."

And that's the game. Time to end the call. "I'll keep that in mind. But right now, I have a meeting to get to. I'll see you Friday night."

"Oh. All right then." Her mother's tone flattened to defeat. "Goodbye, sweetheart."

"Bye, Mother." She hung up the phone and returned her attention to her computer. An image of a blank document mocked her, and with an angry pecking motion, she typed her opening greeting.

Ladies and gentlemen, on behalf of the Delgado Foundation, welcome to the Duke Delgado Awards Ceremony. Tonight,

Her finger paused there, and the cursor blinked its agitation at the lull in activity. Minutes passed—hell, maybe even *days* passed—while she stared at the words, waiting for inspiration and coming up empty.

"Well, this isn't working," she chided herself and reached for the list of property details Val had compiled.

Distracted, she picked up her mug of coffee, took a sip, and immediately grimaced. Blech! Val had warned her the stuff had gone cold. She should have listened. Pushing the cup out of easy reach to the corner of her desk, she buried her concentration in the building sites again.

There had to be a better location than the Loughlin Building somewhere among these sites. She just had to find that golden opportunity in this bunch of numbers and street names. No matter what her mother thought about her work hours, if it took from now 'til Friday, she'd sit here and go through this list with a fine-toothed comb, forgoing food, sleep, and even bathroom breaks.

There was no way in hell she could do business with Jordan Fawcett, even for her beloved foundation. She shuffled through the stapled packets, scanning through the notes she'd made on all the sites they'd visited: one was too small, another difficult for commuters to get to, a third would require rezoning and had included a floor plan that showed massive interior construction needs, meaning they'd be unable to move in for at least a year.

No good. They'd already wasted six months trying to cull together this handful of possibilities. And only one place called to her like a siren's song, the one place she thought perfect, the one place with one great, big imperfection barring her from acquiring it like Godzilla blocking her from her goal.

The Loughlin site. Repped by Jordan Fawcett, her personal Godzilla. If the agent were anyone but him, she'd already have a crew onsite working on the renovations.

She ran a hand through her long hair and swerved her chair to stare out the window again. *Damn you, Jordan, you ran away years ago! Why didn't you stay away? Why did you have to come back and invade my life again?*

When he'd announced he was leaving the Vanguard and her for Houston, *he'd* established the rules of surrender, not her. Now, she'd have to find a way to make sure they both continued to abide by them.

WHEN TEN DAYS WENT by without a word from Val or anyone else at the Delgado Foundation, Jordan figured the building wasn't as perfect for their needs as that insistent board member thought. Either that, or Cam found out he was the agent and wouldn't touch the place because he was involved.

Oh, well. No one could say he hadn't tried. Even Susan would have to admit defeat and let him have the place now.

Regardless of why she'd passed, Cam's radio silence also meant he wouldn't have to see her, which was exactly the way he wanted things between them. He'd spent too many sleepless nights over the last week and a half, trying to convince himself he could do this deal, sit across from her at that board table in her meeting room, connect with her gaze, and remain aloof.

During the day, while his mind stayed occupied with numbers and locations and the day to day challenge of getting around the city in a wheelchair, he could kid himself into believing he'd forgotten all about Cam's laugh, her touch, the scent of her skin. But at night, in bed, staring at the ceiling, his mind chastised him for living in a fantasy world where Cam meant nothing to him. If she didn't matter, his conscience would sneer, why return to New York?

You could have gone anywhere after your football career ended. You could have stayed in Texas, or moved to any other city in the States. Why come back here?

Because you hoped, one day, you'd run into her again.

Not yet, though. Not until he'd made a name for himself in his own chosen profession—without help from family or football. Something she'd never done.

"Hell-o? Jordan? You with us here?"

Jordan glanced up at the prompt and into the eyes of his personal trainer and business partner. The clink of weights and background rock music invaded his musings. Instead of the scent of Cam's skin, rank sweat sharpened the air around him. He shook off thoughts about the bitter past and faced his present.

"Yeah, sorry."

"Come on, dude. Focus. Eight more on each side."

"Right." He lifted the barbell and did his reps, counting aloud after each one, then placed the barbell back on the mat.

"Good," Marcus replied. "Now, the left arm. Remember, you've got two." While Jordan repeated the procedure on his weaker side, Marcus added, "Any news on the site yet?"

"No," he said through huffs and counts. "Which makes me think she's not interested, so we're all good."

Marcus's forehead puckered, and he cocked his head at Jordan. "She who?"

Damn. He hadn't told Marcus about Cam getting first-crack at their building yet. Tightening his grip on the barbells in his hands, he muttered, "There's been a hiccup."

Marcus sat back on his haunches and folded his arms over his chest. "What kind of hiccup?"

He took a deep breath, let the air out slowly. "It seems that Cameron Delgado's foundation has first right of refusal on the Loughlin place."

Marcus shot to his feet, hands balled into fists. "Aw, hell! No wonder you aren't paying attention to me right now. You're in Camland again."

"That's bull!" Jordan dropped the barbells with a loud clank and glared at his friend. "Wait a sec. Camland?"

"Yeah, Camland. Where nothing else matters but Cameron Delgado."

Jordan gave a wry chuckle. "What the hell do you know about Cam? You've never even met her!"

"I didn't have to meet her. From the first time I started working with you in Houston, you've railed about her, cursed her, and used her name as the provocation you needed to push forward when it would've been easier for you to give up."

"I barely even mentioned her."

Marcus snorted. "Yeah, right. Keep telling yourself that, asshole." He switched his seated position, shooting his legs out straight on the mat. "Look, I get it. Everybody's got that one person their heart's obsessed with. You can't help yourself. Your mind replays key scenes at night and makes you wonder, 'If I'd done A instead of B, would we still be together now? If I'd said yes, instead of no...or no, instead of yes. If we'd met five years later or five years earlier, would things be different now?' Cam Delgado's the one your heart's obsessed with. And when we were in Houston, that was fine. I helped you use that obsession to make you stronger, to make you work harder. Even when we came back to New York, I didn't think it would be an issue for you, except to spur you on to get the rehab center going for us. But now, if you're working for her instead—"

Jordan shot up a hand. "Whoa! Back up. I'm *not* working for her. I'm working with the foundation on behalf of HRR."

"Uh-huh." Marcus leaned closer and used his index finger to pull the skin beneath his eyes. "Those dark rings I'm seeing on you? You gonna tell me they have nothing to do with her? Which company are you losing sleep over? Hers or ours?"

Jordan sighed. "Okay, I admit I'm a little distracted with this project for her, but it's not changing the deal you and I have. In fact, it's going to make everything better."

Marcus's lips twisted. "Uh-huh. Right."

"I swear to God, Marcus, the Delgado deal looks pretty much dead in the water. No one over there has called since I faxed the floor plan. I'm betting Cam still wants nothing to do with me, even after all this time. I'm just waiting for Susan to wave the white flag and agree with me. Once that happens, this will all be swept away."

And that would've been great, Jordan thought a few days later, if Susan had cooperated. Unfortunately, late Thursday afternoon, when she called him into her office, he didn't get the reaction he expected.

Anticipation racing high, he rolled down the hall with glee. In just a few minutes, his life would be back on track. He'd call Marcus and tell him they were a go for the property and they could move forward again. At the doorway to her expansive office with its ocean blue walls, cream-colored carpet, and assortment of succulents in white china pots, he stopped and waited for her to grant him admission. She sat at her desk, her head down, gaze burning into her laptop, and her rimless eyeglasses perched precariously on the edge of the bridge of her nose.

He didn't mind that she didn't acknowledge him right away. The pause gave him time to erase delight from showing on his face.

When a full minute passed without any kind of greeting, he rumbled his knuckles on the doorframe. "What's up, Sue?"

She looked up at last, tossed her glasses onto the desktop, and ushered him inside. While he pushed himself forward, she rose from the desk and strode to the door to close it.

Leaning against the door with her arms folded over her chest as if to bar his exit, she demanded, "Are you deliberately screwing up the Delgado deal?"

He'd prepared for this reaction and gave her his best shocked expression. "What?! No. Of course not." In a softer tone, he added, "I told you, Susan. Cam and I didn't part on good terms. So either she still hates me or she's not wild about the property."

Her brick wall posture crumpled. "Where do we stand?"

"Nowhere. I faxed the floorplans to her assistant nearly two weeks ago. At the time, Val said if Cam was interested in acquiring the property, she'd be in touch within a week to ten days."

"Did you follow up with her?"

"Earlier this week, yes." He didn't add that Val had confessed her confusion with her boss's sudden distaste with a property she'd originally thought was ideal.

She pushed away from the door and stalked back to her seat to glare at him at an even level. "And...?"

"And she said they were looking in another direction."

"What other direction?"

He shrugged. "She didn't elaborate."

"And you didn't ask?" Before he could give any kind of reply, she slammed a palm on her desk. "Susan's Rule Number One: Never leave an open-ended deal on the table!"

He bit back his retort about the entirely different number one rule she'd espoused two weeks ago. Six months into his employment here, he'd learned the rules always changed. What remained constant was the fact Susan had a rule for every facet of real estate. At last year's Christmas party, he had joined a bunch of his coworkers in a friendly game of listing off as many of them as they could remember. The game took over an hour.

"Did you try talking to your girlfriend directly?" Susan pressed now. "Did you apologize? Charm her in any way?"

He gave a bitter laugh. "Trust me, Susan. Cam doesn't charm easily."

Susan steepled her fingers in front of her lips. "That's why I assigned this to you. You should know how to get to her. What are you waiting for? I don't care how you do it or what you promise in return. Just get this deal. Need I remind you how much money we're talking about here?"

"No," he muttered. "I'm well aware."

"Then *do* something. Go the extra mile. I assigned this account to you because you know her. You, of all people, should know how to reach her. Think back to when you were dating. If you wanted to wow her, what would you do?"

"I don't—"

She cut him off with an upraised hand. "I'm not asking you. I'm advising you. Whatever that wow thing is, do it, turned up to a hundred. If she likes roses, send her a dozen a day until she says yes. If she loves lobster, charter a plane to fly her to Maine. Does she have a thing for a certain celebrity? Do you know there are services where you can pay to have celebrities record a private message for you? Whatever her thing is, overwhelm her so she'll be incapable of saying no."

Jordan bit his tongue. At one time, he thought he was an expert on Cam's likes and dislikes. Turned out, he was wrong.

"Isn't tomorrow night that dinner fundraiser thing?" Susan asked.

"The Duke Delgado Awards Ceremony." He knew it well, had accompanied her to several over the years they'd dated.

Susan punctuated the air with her index finger. "Yeah, that thing. Figure out a way to get her alone there and talk to her. As a former player for their football team, you should be able to finagle an invitation."

Probably. But since his Vanguard teammates weren't any more thrilled with his abrupt departure from New York than Cam had been, he doubted they'd toss out a welcome mat for his return.

"Take advantage of any insight you have, any string you can pull," Susan suggested. "Beg and plead for her forgiveness, if that's what it takes. Hell, crawl on your belly if you have to. Just get her to buy the property."

Bitter ashes filled his mouth, and he swallowed hard, then grimaced at the taste. "Let's start smaller than that, if you don't mind."

He'd be damned if he'd ever beg Cam for anything ever again.

Chapter 3

"What the hell?" Cam entered the front office to find a forest of roses erupting from her receptionist's desk.

"The delivery kid just dropped them off," Val replied from behind the mélange of ivory-frosted crimson blooms. "*Three dozen* roses for you." Her blond head popped up from behind the garden like a prairie dog's. "I wish some guy was so head-over-heels in love with me, he'd order a bouquet like this and have it delivered to my office where all my coworkers could see and be jealous. Must be nice."

Nice? Not particularly. Even before she pulled the florist's envelope from the plastic stick, Cam had a sneaky suspicion she knew who'd sent the Overkill Bouquet.

"Toss them out." She waved a hand, noticed her ragged nails, and shoved her fists—with the florist's card still clutched between her fingers—into her jacket pockets. "But not here. Take them to the hallway trash. Anywhere in here, and they'll make the whole floor smell like a funeral parlor."

An odor she'd rather not relive in the coming few hours. She had enough reminders to overcome tonight.

"Umm..."

Val's unusual hesitancy ruffled Cam's already frazzled interior. Rising on tiptoes to stretch to full-force-intimidation-six-foot-height, Cam peered over the flowers. What had happened to the competent woman she'd come to admire? Right now, her assistant blushed like a teenager with her first crush.

"Spit it out, Val."

The woman's teddy bear gaze darted in a dozen directions before landing on the ostentatious blooms. "Can I keep them? I mean...you probably get flowers like these all the time...but...well..."

Cam rolled her eyes. *Oh, I so do not have time for this right now. The awards dinner is in six hours. I still have to shower, change, and now it looks like I need an emergency manicure. Why did I let Hank and Luis goad me into shooting pool last night?*

Because her nerves were stretched taut, she needed the stress relief, and she'd assumed a quiet game of pool would be kinder on her hands than a bout of kickboxing. Fool.

As if rubbing salt in Cam's bleeding wounds, Val folded perfect cotton candy-painted fingernails into a clasp of prayer. "Please? I bet they cost a fortune. It'd be a shame to just throw them in the trash."

Annoyance sparked, and for a moment Cam considered using the water in the vase to douse her rising ire. Finally, she sighed. "Put them in the kitchen area until you leave today."

While Val reached eager hands to the cut-glass vase, Cam strode into her office and shut out the world. On the other side of the door, she lifted her purse to eye-level in front of her, dangling it from her fingertips by the thin strap.

Mimicking an announcer's tone, she murmured, "Delgado lines up for the kick."

A quick drop...

A swing of her right leg...

Contact!

Her bag soared through the miniature goalpost standing sentry on the other side of the room. *Da-thump!* The black canvas clutch landed in a small vinyl storage box sitting directly behind a pair of white plastic uprights on the carpeted end zone.

"A perfect extra-pointer," she exclaimed in her best sportscaster voice. "And *that's* the game!"

Exhaling air to imitate the sound of a roaring crowd, she shimmied to her desk in a victory dance. When she sat in her office chair, the ergonomic hiss was a welcome sound in her inner sanctum. She pulled the florist's card from her pocket. The envelope displayed the name of a high-priced Manhattan flower boutique. When she removed the cardboard square, the words kinked her stomach in spirals of torment.

Please don't let our past ruin what could be a bright future for hundreds of kids. Your dad wouldn't want that to be his legacy. Call me.

-Jordan

Her gaze strayed to the gilt-framed photo on the corner of her desk. Daddy's smiling face, shadowed by the football helmet askew on his head, stared back. Almost thirty years had passed since that horrible night. Yet, she still heard her mother weeping, still felt that gnawing hunger in her belly, still shivered as icy realization clutched her heart.

The dire words floated through a miasmic sea of memories.

"... storm over Guadalupe... "

"... plane went down... "

"... rain forest... "

"... no survivors... "

The tiny white envelope fluttered to her desktop.

How dare he? Jordan Fawcett, the one man she'd ever dared to let into her private life, the man who'd betrayed her, insisted on trying to do business with her. And now he thought he could use the memory of her beloved father to goad her into submission. As if nothing had ever happened between them. He actually thought a couple of dozen roses and some pointed reminders on a card smaller than the business ones she kept on her desk would make up for her heartbreak, for her inability to trust any other man, for the self-doubts that plagued her to this day.

"Sorry, Jordan." She tore the card once, twice, a dozen times until pieces of white cardboard confetti littered her scarlet pencil skirt. "Go play on someone else's field. I'll figure out a way to win this game without you."

Problem was, deep inside her brain, a shadowy voice kept saying he was right.

JORDAN HUDDLED OUTSIDE the gated alleyway. The rain, a light drizzle all afternoon, had become a deluge. Sheets of icy water streamed from the black sky, carving a path between the collar of his raincoat and his shirt, dousing his back until fabric stuck to his skin like pilot fish on a shark.

Thunder rumbled overhead and seconds later, a spear of lightning pierced the night. Great. Just what he needed. New York City, particularly this stretch of Manhattan's Upper West Side, was a pain in his butt. With no parking available on the street, he couldn't sit in his van. Thanks to the mayor's Clean Streets

Initiative, loiterers were quickly (and quietly) arrested before the hoity-toity residents might clap eyes on them. God forbid their sensibilities become offended by having to look upon the huddled masses.

Of all the stupid ideas he could've acted upon…

He supposed his name and past triumphs would have gained him entry into the honorary dinner tonight. If he'd attended the awards gala, he probably would have found an opportunity to corner her alone in some quiet alcove, instead of here on the street. But there, he'd also have to contend with a host of angry pro football players acting as bodyguards.

The players from the New York Vanguard, both active and retired, considered Cameron Delgado their lucky charm, their mascot, their Little Orphan Annie. Long before the wreckage of Duke's plane was discovered, his daughter was a media magnet, based on her birth alone. After Duke's demise, however, his former teammates immediately went into protective mode, closed ranks, and blocked her from the spotlight, with Bertie Wallace the biggest Papa Bear of all.

Fifteen years later, when the foundation held its annual Duke Awards ceremony and fundraiser for the Delgado Foundation, there was the fatherless waif, now fully grown and controlling the reins of Duke's massive financial empire. With a shiny new MBA from Wharton and a corral of young and old football players surrounding her, Cameron Delgado claimed her place as the league's princess. And there she remained.

While struggling to make a name for himself in the pros, Jordan had been so focused on his career he hadn't given much thought to some dead has-been's foundation for needy children around the world. But he'd noticed *her*, and he'd done everything he could think of to get her to notice him. They'd been the perfect couple—until he'd gone for broke and proposed. That was when it all went to crap.

Tires hushed over wet pavement, and a black limousine pulled to a stop outside the sleek, modern building.

Thank God. He pushed himself forward out of the shadows, but remained far enough back that he stayed invisible to anyone standing on the sidewalk.

The green-coated, white-gloved doorman reached for the handle of the passenger door while simultaneously opening a black umbrella. Out stepped a pair of shapely legs, tanned and supple, shod in strappy black shoes. Rhinestone clips near the toes glinted beneath the streetlights.

Time to get this show on the road.

Rolling forward, he held out his hand. "Darling! I'm sorry I'm late. Traffic was brutal."

Cam stood on the sidewalk, the car door yawning open behind her. Crap, he'd forgotten how tall she was. An average woman's height worked against him these days, thanks to the chair, but in comparison to Cameron Delgado, he might as well be a Lilliputian. Yet, despite her six-foot frame, she always looked delicate and lovely in dresses and heels when he knew damn well she was meaner and stronger than a linebacker.

Judging by the disgusted expression that crept over her face, she saw him as a pile of dog crap on the bottom of her shoe.

"You should have called, honey," she purred.

Without missing a beat or disclosing any revulsion in her tone, she leaned low enough to kiss his cheek. Her cologne, lightly floral with a hint of musk, tickled his nostrils and evoked memories of long ago days filled with laughter.

A sharp pang of regret pierced his chest. Maybe she had run scared that afternoon, but he'd screwed the follow-up—badly. If he had stayed with her, had never left for Houston, would they have found their way back together by now? Would he still have the use of his legs? A thriving football career? Hell, for all he knew, she might have already discarded him for another husband, following in the footsteps of her illustrious mother.

The doorman, hovering with the umbrella, also leaned closer, and the rainwater flowed over the convex edge directly onto Jordan's head to shock him back to the here and now.

"When you didn't show," Cam added, straightening to her full height again. "I made other plans."

As a final insult, she ruffled his sodden hair through her fingers before turning away, effectively dismissing him. Her familiar laughter, this time filled with derision, rang over the clack of her heels as she strode into the apartment building, the doorman running to keep up with her fabulous, long, *perfect* legs.

Chapter 4

The elevator whooshed Cam up to the penthouse suite while she struggled to rein in her skittering nerves and remain on her feet.

Oh, God. Jordan. Here. Outside her building. Waiting for her...

The door slid open into her living room, and she stumbled to the couch, peeling off her raincoat along the way. By the time she collapsed into the plush gray cushions, the trembling in her legs had made any further movement impossible. Tears filled her eyes, and she sniffed them back to keep her makeup in place. The Duke Awards, an annual fundraiser and celebration of her father's life, always ripped her emotions apart. Drafting and giving her speech every year made her antsy. Greeting all the most famous names in professional sports who attended the event exhausted her. The endless reminders of her father and his generosity brought on melancholy. Watching her mother dancing with the man she'd married last year riled her. So many emotions whirled inside her. Everywhere she turned, everything that met her gaze, evoked some kind of physical reaction.

Tonight, though, coming face-to-face with Jordan seated in that wheelchair, left her an overwrought mess. Yes, she *hated* him, but she couldn't help indulging in a teeny bout of sympathy at how cruelly fate had treated him after their breakup. She hadn't seen him in person since before the injury that ruined his career. She'd seen the game, of course. Two years after he left the Vanguard franchise to sign with the Houston Privateers, a blitz by the defensive line resulted in him being sacked, the hit from three players at once so hard it damaged his lower spine.

Regardless of the hard feelings she'd nursed over his abrupt departure, she had immediately flown to Texas to help him in any way she could. Hospital security had refused to let her in.

Then, she spotted Paris Redmond glide by the front desk with a smile and a wave in the guard's direction, and her heart sank. Without a word passing between them, Cam knew exactly where she stood, physically and romantically, in Jordan's life. By putting her on his no admittance list, he had tattooed his ambivalence directly onto her heart.

Now, bad enough he was back in New York with a new career, a new look, and a new way of getting around in the world. Even after the flowers and the phone calls he'd left with Val, she never thought he'd have the nerve to show up here. To pitch his property, face-to-face.

Another thought struck her, this one razor-sharp. Was Paris with him?

Did it matter? she asked herself.

Not really.

On a deep sigh of regret, Cam removed her shoes and flexed her aching toes, then let her body go limp, boneless. She flung one arm over her head to shield her eyes from the overhead lights. God, she was a mess tonight! Wired as she was after the annual homage to her dad, toss in Jordan's sudden appearance in front of her building, and no wonder her skin felt electrically charged and too tight for her frame. She needed a hot bath, an enormous glass of wine, and a friend to talk to.

Problem was, she didn't have the energy to move. She dug into her teeny silver evening purse to grab her cell. Only one person she could call right now, and she didn't hesitate, regardless of the hour.

The phone on the other end rang once before his cheery voice said, "What took you so long? I've been waiting for details all night."

"Feel like popping over for a while?"

"That bad, huh? Don't worry, sweetheart. I'm on my way."

"Thanks. I'll see you in ten." Cam disconnected the call, dropped her phone on the cushion beside her, and closed her eyes. Without moving, she announced up toward the ceiling, "Call front desk."

A buzz sounded in the room, and the familiar voice of the overnight manager, Tommy, intoned over the loudspeaker recessed in the ceiling's corner. "Good evening, Ms. Delgado. How may I help you?"

"Hi, Tommy. Mr. Wallace is coming over. Send him up right away when he arrives."

"Yes, Ms. Delgado."

"Thanks."

"You're very welcome. Enjoy your evening." The speaker clicked off, and Cam sat alone with her thoughts again.

After several minutes of blissful silence, the bell dinged, announcing the elevator's arrival on her private floor. Rousing her tired synapses, she pushed herself to her bare and aching feet. That one action sapped what remained of her dwindling energy, and she stayed rooted to the floor.

The steel door whooshed open, and a grizzled bear of a man lumbered inside, arms extended. He reached her in half a dozen strides and swooped her into a hug.

"There's my beautiful lady," he crooned in her ear as he squeezed the breath out of her lungs. "Was it that bad?"

"No worse than usual." She wriggled out of his embrace to restart her respiratory system. "The same people, the same conversations..." On a huff of expelled air, she flounced back onto the sofa. "You know how this shindig plays out."

For several years, until his divorce from her mother, he'd been an active participant like her. After the divorce, vindictive Mom made sure he never again made the guest list—despite his position as Daddy's best friend and head coach of the team they once both carried to so many game wins. He probably could've attended the annual fete anyway. The team would have backed him up, but Bertie, the peacemaker, would never publicly humiliate her mother that way. He always saw the best in everyone, even his ex-wife.

"Well, something's got you wound up tonight," he remarked. "What is it? Did your mom start in on you again?"

"No. She was too involved with Mr. Ellison to notice me." Mr. Ellison. Husband number...four?... five?... since Daddy died? She couldn't keep track. Only Bertie mattered to her. Husband number two, the man she'd always consider her only stepfather, no matter how many men married her mother in the coming years.

Bertie gave her a meaningful once-over from head to toe and snorted. "Looking as gorgeous as you do in that outfit? How could anyone ignore you?"

Despite her mangled emotions, she mustered a smile. "Ha. Easy, with perfect-size-two Mom in the room."

He skimmed an index finger down her nose, the way he always did when she was an insecure child with a gorgeous mother who judged her too harshly. "There's more to you than a dress size, beautiful. Remember that." He emphasized the reminder with a poke on the tip of her nose.

She wriggled on the couch, folding her arms over her chest to camouflage the bit of bulge at her waistline that no hydraulic underwear could hide.

"Stop that," he growled, pulling her arms apart. "You're perfect, Cam. A real man likes a woman with curves."

A block of tears clogged her throat, and she swallowed them back, then patted the space beside her. Her palm slapped the slender chain of her evening bag, and she wrapped her fingers around the cool silver links before flinging the accessory over the back of the couch. A clink-thud erupted when the purse hit the polished wooden floor.

"Sit," she said, her voice rough as sandpaper. "I need your shoulder."

"Uh-oh." He settled next to her, his bulk sinking the cushion so that she rose a tick—no small feat, considering her own meatiness. She frowned, and Bertie wrapped a brawny arm around her to bring her closer. His every inhale and exhale echoed against her ribcage, a soothing tempo she'd enjoyed since childhood. She let the rhythm calm her frazzled nerve endings, snuggling closer, her ear pressed to his chest until his vibrato broke the spell. "So... what's up?"

On a weighty sigh, she straightened again, mentally scrambling to figure out where to begin. "Okay, so you know how I've been trying to find a new space for the midtown center?"

"Uh-huh..."

One of the many things she loved about Bertie, he never pressed her or interrupted when she needed to talk. He always let her move at her own pace.

"Well, there's a building about five blocks from our current site that looks perfect. Plenty of space for our growing pains, convenient to bus and subway stops, and in our price range."

"But..."

She uttered the statement in one breath, without a pause. "But the real estate agent is Jordan Fawcett."

Bertie gave a curt nod. "Ah."

"Yeah." She grimaced.

She didn't have to say anything more about her feelings. Without additional details, Bertie understood how painful this situation was for her. After all, he'd been the one to fly to Texas to help gather up her shattered pieces when Jordan rejected her at the hospital. Not her mother—*never* her mother—whose only advice was the constant, "If you'd only lose some weight, you could have your pick of men." Like she could fight the genetics that made her build more like Duke Delgado's instead of the frail-bird-stature of her mother's family.

"Why do I sense you've got more to say?"

Good old astute Bertie. She tangled her hands in the fabric of her skirt. "Because I do. Guess who was waiting for me outside the building when I came home tonight."

His lantern jaw unhinged and hung open. "No."

She nodded.

"How'd he look?"

"Wet," she retorted. "He must have hung outside here for hours, waiting for me."

"Well, that's interesting."

"Ya think? I find it idiotic. He could wind up with pneumonia."

He quirked a brow. "Would you care if he did?"

"Of course I would." She punched a fist into the throw pillow beside her. "Do you have any idea how much damage a diagnosis like that could do to a man in his physical condition?" He gave her a scrutinizing look, and heat crept into her cheeks. "Yeah, okay. I looked it up."

His eyes bored into her over-exhausted brain. "Uh-huh. Care to tell me why?"

She waved her hand, partly in dismissal, but also to cool her face. "It was ages ago. When he was first injured. I wanted to know more about his condition, what changes he had to make in his life." God, she sounded like a stalker. "I was worried about him, okay? He and I were close for years. We almost got married. I can't just turn off my concerns because he ditched me. I mean, I'm not as heartless as my mother."

"Your mother's not heartless. She's had to be strong her whole life. It's made her..." He paused, searching for the right word. "...tougher than most people take her for. She's got a soft, gooey center—like you, and some cretins have taken advantage of that. So she's learned to hide that part of her. You haven't, and she dreads the idea you might be hurt the way she was."

Yeah, right. Cam sniffed. The only softness in Mom came from the finest skin care regimen money could buy. "I will never understand how you can continue to defend her."

"We all have our flaws, sweetheart." He poked her nose again. "Including you. But we've gotten off-topic. We were talking about Jordan. I guess he really wanted to see you, so he must've thought it worth the risk of pneumonia. I mean, he could've called the corporate office if it was about showing the property. But, no. He hung around here in the rain."

"Yeah." She gazed up at the ceiling, unable to look him in the eye. "About that."

"Ah," he repeated with the same realized inflection. "He did call the corporate office. I take it you initiated the correspondence about the building before you knew the identity of the agent in charge of the property. So, how many times after that initial interest did you pass him off onto Val?"

She shrugged. "Val took the original call. I've had no contact with him at all. As soon as I realized he was the selling agent, I told her to forget it."

"Okay, let me get this straight. He's got a property that's ideal for your needs, a property that could make a helluva commission for its agent, but once you discovered Jordan was the agent, you had Val go radio silent on him. Did you think he wouldn't try to follow up?"

Realizing this was a rhetorical question, she didn't answer. What could she say?

"Well, if you refused to take his calls, it's no wonder he tried to talk to you here. You should've expected it. What'd he say when he saw you?"

The message on the card from this afternoon's floral arrangement, burned into her memory, came to her lips unbidden. "He said I shouldn't let our ugly history affect Daddy's legacy."

"Hmm..." He scratched his temple. "Not exactly the apology I would've expected from him."

"Why would he apologize? Nothing's changed. I'm still the fat girl he ditched for a beauty queen when he realized dating Duke Delgado's daughter wouldn't propel his career into the stratosphere. Now that he's no longer playing ball, he thinks he can bounce back into my life and use me to up his real estate creds. Like I'm some kind of big-girl trampoline."

See? She wasn't as soft and gooey as Bertie thought. She saw right through Jordan's game.

Bertie shook his head. "I can't believe I was so wrong about him. I always thought better of Jordan."

"So did I—once. Now, I know he's a user and a creep." Her voice cracked on the last word as the pain pierced her heart yet again, as it always did when she thought about the man she'd once loved. Despite her exhaustion, she tightened her frame as if braced for battle.

If Bertie noticed, he didn't remark on her sudden stiffness beside him. "At least tell me you got in the last word with the bum."

"I did."

He gave her shoulder a quick squeeze. "That's my warrior woman. Now, you listen to me. No matter what you decide to do about the midtown center, your dad's legacy is safe in your hands and always has been. If you really like the space, go for it. Unless your bitterness won't be happy until he's penniless and sleeping in the street..."

"That's not it at all! You know me better than that." She dropped her gaze to her hands, wringing them in her lap. "The truth is, I don't think I relish sitting across a board table from him, Bertie. I mean, when I saw him tonight, trapped in that chair, I felt so bad I wanted to cry. I don't think I could work with him and maintain my composure."

"I'll do it if you can't. Frankly, I'd welcome the opportunity to give him a piece of my mind. Despite your history, he owed you better than what you got in Houston. Say the word, and I'll take over the acquisition."

"And let him think I'm still so hung up on him that I can't face him over a business deal?" God, wouldn't *that* be humiliating! "No, thanks. I'll handle him, and I'll get that property. By the time I'm done with him, he'll wish he'd stayed in Houston. If I have to, I'll kick his ass back there." She mimed dropping a ball and kicking it over the goal posts.

With a low chuckle, Bertie kissed her cheek. "I know you will."

JORDAN HAD PLENTY OF time to review the evening's events when he returned home. After a hot shower, a warm towel, and dry clothes, he would've expected sleep to overtake him easily. But, no. In bed, he stared at the ceiling, reviewing the mistakes he'd made in trying to reach Cameron. He'd really underestimated the power of his charms. Why was *she* so mad at *him* anyway?

Okay, so maybe they hadn't parted under the best of circumstances, but he would have always lived under her father's shadow if he'd remained with the Vanguard. Regardless of his success on the gridiron, the whispers that he only had his position because he was dating Duke's daughter—his *coach's* stepdaughter—had grown too loud to ignore. So when the Houston Privateers sought a veteran quarterback to provide leadership for their group of young, talented but inexperienced players, Paris pitched him as the perfect candidate. Lucky for him, the Privateers agreed, and he signed on the dotted line without consulting Cam.

As soon as she heard, she shut down, broke off all communications, and cut him out of her life. He should have realized her loyalty would always remain with the Vanguard. Daddy's girl, Daddy's team.

God help him, he still wanted her. Seeing her had been a big mistake. Bad enough he'd ceded home court advantage, but then she looked down on him from her dressy sky-high heels, making him feel vulnerable and small with one glare. A devastating fall when she was the one person who'd always looked up to him in the past...

Once again, as Marcus had predicted, the what-ifs invaded his thoughts. If he hadn't signed the Houston contract, how would their lives have turned out?

Would he have taken the hit that destroyed his pro career during a different game? And if he had been injured while still playing for the Vanguard, would she have cared enough to come back to him? Or would she have kept him on her cut list, the way her mother treated Bertie? Persona non grata.

He shuddered. Big mistake, he chided himself again, going to her apartment building tonight. *Huge*, honking mistake. She was always brittle after the annual awards dinner, primarily because Bertie couldn't attend and Bertie was her primary shelter from most storms. Jordan should've remembered how, whenever *he'd* accompanied her to the yearly fete while they were dating, she'd cling to him all night, and then, at the end of the evening, she'd collapse in his arms and weep herself dry. Why hadn't he remembered that?

He spent most of the night mentally kicking himself for his lack of empathy, for forgetting how fragile she could be. Had he imagined that haunted look in her eyes? Recalled it from some past evening when he'd been the man to soothe her tumult after a similar event? Had she really laughed, or was the sound he'd heard before she disappeared inside been more a bitten-back sob?

Sleep evaded him, refusing to allow him any respite from his conflicting thoughts.

The next morning, bleary-eyed and irritable, he rolled into his office only to spot his boss waiting at the reception desk, wearing a grin wide enough to eat the Cheshire Cat. Susan veered around the desk, clapping in short bursts. "Congratulations, Jordan."

"For what?" he grumbled. Was he about to get the boot for not earning that double commission she so prized?

"We just got a call from the Delgado Foundation. They want to set up a time to meet and discuss the acquisition."

Shock jolted inside him. "Is this a joke?"

She shook her head and held out an index card. "Cameron Delgado asked to speak with you specifically. No one else."

He grabbed the card and stared at the numbers and letters written in the usual felt tip marker. As the words infiltrated his muddy brain, he looked up at Susan. "That's Cam Delgado's direct line?"

"Uh-huh. She called first thing this morning. I didn't even have a chance to stow my purse before I was writing down all the particulars. How'd you convince her? Was it the roses? I told you. No woman can resist three dozen red and white roses."

He left Susan to prattle on and take credit for his breakthrough while he pushed himself into his office. The truth was, he had no idea what made Cam change her mind, but he doubted *a thousand* flowers would have affected the ice princess he saw last night.

For God's sake, she'd ruffled his hair—like he was a street urchin in a Dickens Christmas play. Tiny Tim, all grown up and still a lame beggar. A ball of bile rose in his throat, and he swallowed hard while closing his office door. The bitter aftertaste made him grimace. He removed his jacket, hung it on the low hook set on the coat rack in the corner, then made himself comfortable behind his desk, leaving the index card atop the folder with the building's info at the side of his keyboard and monitor. As he stared out the window at the traffic on the avenue five stories below him, a sharp rap sounded on his door. The office receptionist, Rachel, swept in with a steaming mug of coffee.

She placed the white ceramic mug on his desk next to the folder.

"I've told you before, you don't have to do that," he said.

Shrugging, she stepped away. "If I'm getting one for me, it's rude to not get one for you at the same time."

He gave her a disgruntled look. "You don't drink coffee."

"Maybe not right now, but I'm trying to acquire a taste for it."

He stifled the urge to shout that he didn't need her pity, but he understood she meant well. She wanted to help without embarrassing him. While her intentions were noble, he resented she felt the need to take care of him without letting him know she was taking care of him. As if he wasn't aware of his limitations. Still, he couldn't get angry.

He'd spent the first six months of his recovery lashing out at everyone who came near with an outstretched hand. Only intense counseling had reminded him that assistance, whether wanted or not, indicated people cared. And he couldn't punish them for caring, or in Cam's case, for *not* caring.

"Thanks, Rache," he said instead.

She smiled. "Any time. Besides, you're gonna need the caffeine. Don't forget. You've got a ten o'clock with Ernest Tallmadge."

He groaned. "Right." Ernest Tallmadge owned a string of laundromats and was seeking a site in SoHo to open a new one. The man was a whirling dervish of brawn, astute business acumen, and endless energy. He didn't believe in cutting Jordan any slack just because he was confined to a wheelchair.

The irony didn't escape Jordan's sense of humor. While he often resented Rachel's habit of treating him with gentle consideration, he also grew annoyed with Tallmadge for not allowing him some small concession.

Once Rachel left and closed the door again, he sipped the brew while going through the papers in the Delgado folder. When he finally had a handle on what he planned to say, he picked up the phone and called the number on the top of the card. To his surprise, she answered on half a ring.

"Delgado Foundation, this is Cameron."

"You answer your own phone. How...down-to-earth of you." He could've bitten his tongue the second the scathing remark left his lips. No sleep and a hectic runaround meeting to commence within an hour made him more obnoxious than usual. Or maybe Cam brought out the worst in him.

"I also negotiate my own deals," she shot back. "So, when it comes to investing the foundation's money, no matter how large or small a sum, I answer my phone. How are you, Jordan? It was good to see you last night. You should have contacted me earlier. I would have made sure you were on the guest list for the gala. I'd imagine many of your former teammates would've loved to see you again."

Was that a verbal slap? A reminder of the hard feelings he'd engendered when he'd left the Vanguard team so precipitously? He gritted his teeth, biting back a quick retort for the second time in as many minutes. He didn't want to spar with her. He wanted a deal. But a little drawn blood might gain him the upper hand after last night's hair rustling incident.

"How's your mother, Cam?"

Thwap! The ball landed in her court again. A sharp hiss on the other end of the phone told him he'd aced her.

"She's fine. She remarried last year. Andrew Ellison. He's the CEO of Cooper Industries. They make... widgets or something. I don't know."

The tension in her tone didn't escape Jordan's notice and for a moment, he felt a pang of sympathy. He hadn't heard about the new marriage, and her mention of another wedding for the Delgado widow sliced too close to the bone for comfort.

If Cam was the ice princess, her mother, Laurel, was the fiery dragon who imprisoned her daughter in a tower of insecurity and crippling self-hate. Laurel Delgado Wallace Kiernan Moffit now-Ellison had spent decades beating down Cam's self-esteem until she never felt good enough for any man's affections. Not even the one who swore he'd love her forever and backed it up with a perfect square-cut solitaire. He still had the ring, tucked in the breast pocket of the suit he'd worn that night and never put on again. Was it any wonder he wanted to put distance between them after that humiliation?

Nowadays, only Bertie built up her confidence, kept her grounded, and gave her the unconditional love she'd missed since Duke's death.

"Be sure to send your mother my congratulations," he said with a tinge of acid charring the words.

"I will."

A heavy silence fell between them. He could almost picture her in her office, pacing the wide open space behind the desk where the wall of windows looked out over the East River. She rarely sat still, even when in a good mood, and the topic of Laurel always riled her into frenetic activity.

He struggled to come up with something else to say to her, something that would remove the specter of her mother from their conversation. When they dated, whenever Cam was all wound up after going a few rounds with Laurel over something stupid, he'd take her to their "quiet place." Inwood Hill Park, a forest in the city, had hiking trails and salt marshes and forests, all perfect for burning excess energy, finding peace, or screaming into the void, depending upon her need at the time.

His hands gripped the handles of his chair. He would never again be able to indulge her need for that level of physical activity. No wonder she wanted nothing to do with him after his injury.

Face it, Jordan. You're useless to her now.

"So..." she said at last. "...that building."

He shook off his self-pity. "Right. Have you seen the property yet?"

"The exterior. And I've reviewed the floorplans you faxed over."

Of course she had. Cam never did anything half-assed. She hated surprises and probably spent as much time digging into the details of the building as Susan had.

"I do want to see the interior for myself so I can gauge the changes we'll need to incorporate to make the site suitable for our specific needs. And I'll be bringing my construction manager with me. We need to review specs and figure out costs on our end."

Her cool, crisp timbre showed no indication they'd once shared a past and dreamed of a shared future. He doodled curlicues on the back of the index card to feign indifference, the closest he could come to matching her tone. "Of course. When would be convenient for you?"

"The sooner the better, honestly. I don't want to waste your time or mine if the site can't be modified within my budget."

Ha. Small countries didn't have *half* the foundation's budget. He left that particular comment unsaid. "I can meet you there later this afternoon or tomorrow. Which do you prefer?"

"Tomorrow would be fine, thanks. Shall we say three o'clock?"

With a few taps of the keyboard, he pulled up a copy of his calendar. His afternoon was completely open—a fact he had no intention of divulging to her. The last thing he'd allow her to feel for him was pity. "I'll shuffle a few appointments around to make it work," he lied.

"I'd appreciate that. Thank you."

"You're welcome." God, they sounded so stiff with each other! Hard to believe they'd once been intimate.

"Terrific. I'll see you then. Goodbye."

He said his own goodbye and pressed the disconnect button, but kept the receiver cradled near his ear. How shortsighted of him to not realize she'd be in charge of this deal. He had assumed once he got her okay to move forward, he'd be dealing with her army of lawyers and accountants. He'd forgotten Cam was a hands-on kind of girl, in all aspects of her life. His mind traveled back to days when those hands had touched him, delighted him, relaxed him.

Dammit, how was he supposed to work with her on a regular basis and not let his resentment leech out all over their dealings? He'd need someone to run interference. Before he could chicken out, he dialed a number he never expected to have to call again.

After only two rings, a silky-voiced receptionist answered.

"I'd like to speak to Mr. Wallace, please," he said. "Tell him it's Jordan Fawcett."

A few minutes later, Bertie growled into the phone, "I was wondering how long you'd wait to call me."

Thrilled the old goat was willing to even speak to him these days, Jordan stifled a sigh of relief. "How are you, Bertie?"

"Curious, mostly."

Yeah, that made two of them.

"I'm not going to talk about whatever's gone on between you and Cam, so if you're calling to badmouth my girl or tell me your side of the story, we can hang up now."

Nice to see Bertie hadn't changed in the last several years. He was still the same no-nonsense curmudgeon. "Fair enough. I'll cut to the chase. Has she told you about the Loughlin building?"

"Is that the place the foundation's looking at over on West Fifteenth? Yeah, she's mentioned it. But you know I have nothing to do with the day-to-day running of the foundation."

"No, but you have a lot to do with the day-to-day of Cam."

"And she's off-limits in this conversation, so unless you wanna talk football, I'm gonna hang up. I've got two dozen players waiting for me down on the field. Welcome back to New York, Jordie, but I got stuff to do, so adios for now."

A fumbling on the other end had Jordan mentally scrambling while he shouted into the phone, "Wait, wait! Don't hang up!"

Crap. Bertie was Jordan's only insight into Cameron's mindset. So if the old coot wanted to talk football, he'd have to figure out a way to talk about Cam while talking about football. At least, that was the way he *thought* Bertie wanted to play this conversation. His brain scurried for a connection.

"Time's wastin', Jordan."

At last, he sighed and opted for the lamest excuse in the playbook. "Okay, so, here's the deal. I've been thinking about this game from a couple of years ago and wondering where I might've gone wrong. It was the fourth quarter, and we were down by six." Probably more like forty, but he'd keep the score close for the mock scenario. "Their defense was a solid wall, and I couldn't seem to get the offense to move forward enough to get a first down. I tried everything to get around them. Nothing worked. On the third down with minutes to go, I went with a Statue of Liberty play and tried to draw the defense's attention elsewhere, but they saw right through it. I lost the game. It's been running through my head lately, and I need to know. If you were me, in that situation, what would you have done?"

Expelled breath whooshed through the earpiece. "Well, now, son, that's hard to say. What I can tell you is that a Statue of Liberty is a pretty expected play these days. But you know what no one ever expects to see? A fumblerooski. Whatever happened to a good old fumblerooski?"

"I have no idea."

Oh, he knew the fumblerooski, a play of misdirection where a QB placed the football on the ground as if fumbled, then the offense tricked the defense into following the wrong player downfield while the real ball carrier headed in a different direction. The idea was to gain as much yardage as possible before the opposing team noticed they were chasing the wrong guy.

And while he could perfectly diagram the play, he had no clue how it pertained to his problem with Cam.

Who was the quarterback in this fumblerooski?

Him? Or...her?

Chapter 5

Cam took extra care with her appearance the next day. Jordan knew all her ugliest secrets and wouldn't be afraid to use them to throw her off her game. His "fond regards" toward her mom yesterday told her he wasn't above playing dirty. God knew why, but he wanted to bust her chops.

Mom always said, "Your clothes are your armor." *So, okay. Let's see what protective gear I can find in my closet.*

She chose a pair of soft, suede leggings in a fawn hue, spiked leather boots in a darker brown that came just to her knees, and a cream-colored blouse, which she planned to pair with a maroon blazer. Studying her image in the full-length mirror in her bedroom, she tried to draw up a veneer of confidence. On the outside, she might look like a woman in control, but inside, her soft heart had melted to mush and her nerves bristled at the thought of seeing Jordan again.

Face it, honey. You never got over him.

Tears stung her eyes, and she turned away from her reflection before they fell and stained her cheeks. She couldn't do this, couldn't stand beside him and pretend she didn't care. Every emotion she felt for him, all the love she still harbored, would show on her face, no matter what color blazer she wore.

Had he ever loved her? Or was she just his entry into professional football society, easily discarded when she'd served her purpose? If the latter were true, why would he have asked her to marry him?

Her mother's sneering voice echoed in her skull. *You should have accepted his proposal. A girl of your size won't get that many opportunities to get married. You're too big, too masculine. Men like their women small and dainty. Feminine. You can put an evening gown and flawless makeup on a pig, but it's still a pig.*

"Thanks, Mom." She pressed her nose up and snorted.

She didn't regret turning down Jordan's proposal years ago, regardless of her mother's prediction about her looming spinsterhood. She'd simply not been ready to roll those ugly dice, and avoiding long-term loneliness seemed a stupid reason to say yes.

The first teardrop landed on her sleeve, leaving a blot of tinted moisturizer on the cuff. "Dammit!" Now, she'd have to change her outfit *and* redo her makeup. Frustration released the tap, and her tears fell in earnest.

She grabbed a moist wipe from her vanity and proceeded to scrub her face clean. Defeat settled on her shoulders, heavy and debilitating. Legs weak and shaky, Cam collapsed on her bed, prepared to call Bertie to tell him to go to the meeting in her place.

No.

She couldn't give Jordan the satisfaction.

On a deep breath, she unbuttoned and whipped off the shirt, tossing it in the corner. The boots came off next, followed by her socks and her pants. In just her underwear, she strode to the full-length mirror and stared levelly at her reflection. She didn't need clothes to be her armor. *She* was her armor. Her business acumen, her experience, her intelligence, her quick wit, she was the whole package.

Screw her clothes, screw her broad shoulders and her excessive height, and her cellulite thighs and her nowhere-near-flat belly. If any man couldn't handle all of her the way she was, including Jordan, they didn't deserve any of her. She was also tough enough to take advantage of their vulnerability.

Fired up, she headed to her walk-in closet and looked through the garments hanging there. She wouldn't dress for Jordan. She intended to dress for *her*.

An hour later, she stood outside the building she hoped to acquire, her construction supervisor, Antonio Marrone, at her side. She wore a pink-and-green floral flared A dress with a hot pink jacket and pink suede ankle boots. Whenever the breeze picked up, the skirt fluttered around her legs. The ensemble made her feel fun and pretty, and brought a smile to her lips. She wouldn't apologize for eschewing staid business attire for a spot of color to cheer her dreary mood. Nor would she dress to fade into the background or to appear smaller, as her mother and society often demanded.

Jordan arrived at three-fifteen, rolled his wheelchair up the sidewalk, gave her the once-over, and exclaimed, "Wow! You look great, Cam. What's the occasion?"

Already annoyed at his tardiness, she didn't appreciate the comment—as if she needed to explain her wardrobe to him or anyone, for that matter. With a toss of her hair, she replied, "No occasion. You're late."

"Yeah, sorry. Some idiot truck driver used the handicapped spaces in the back lot as a loading dock. He decided to take a stroll to the bodega down the street for some coffee while the restaurant crew unloaded a month's worth of beef from the back. Took the keys with him, so I had to wait 'til he came back, settled up with the restaurant's manager, and finally moved the truck out of the space before I could pull in and park. It's not easy being in a chair in the city, between the lack of viable options to maneuver around and the inconsiderate buttholes who don't care if they inconvenience others as long as they shave five minutes off their busy schedules."

"So then why live here? You could manage real estate anywhere."

His brows drew downward in an expression of repressed fury. "Wow. Way to minimize my 'little' job, eh? It's not like I run a multi-million dollar foundation, right?"

Heat flared in her cheeks. "I didn't say that. All I meant was—"

"Ahem!" Antonio cut in. "Maybe we could go inside, rather than continuing arguing here on the street?"

Cam clamped her jaws shut. She had to remember why she was here. She and Jordan had to put their personal animosities aside if they hoped to make this deal work. She *wanted* this building, and judging by Jordan's relentless pursuit, he wanted her to acquire it. So, why couldn't they behave around each other long enough to make their one common goal happen? Would they always wind up sniping over stupid comments, each of them taking offense at the most innocuous statements? Well, she'd try to remain impassive and hope he followed her lead.

"You're right, Antonio. Jordan, I apologize. Shall we?" She waved toward the locked door and stepped aside to give him a wide berth for his chair to roll through.

He pushed himself closer and held out the key to her. "Would you like to do the honors?"

She glanced at the door and noted the lock sat a good foot above the latch, probably out of Jordan's reach. Her annoyance ebbed away, and a sliver of pity pierced her heart. No wonder he was so bitter. Things she took for granted—unlocking a door, finding a parking spot, or even dashing into a bodega for a bottle of water or a bag of chips—required planning and assistance for him.

A man as physical and independent as Jordan used to be would probably find making the adjustment devastating.

"Sure." She took the key and inserted it into the lock.

With Antonio's help, she pushed open the heavy steel door.

"Light switch is on your left," Jordan said as they went inside.

Antonio reached over, and with a click, the interior flooded with light. The empty space seemed massive, but Cam imagined the doorways to classrooms, the laughter of children and teens filling the emptiness.

They moved deeper into the vast open area, and Antonio let out a low whistle. "Nice place. Looks like it's a good size, lots of natural light. I'm gonna go check out the wiring." He leaned closer to her to whisper, "You okay down here with him?" Cam nodded, and Antonio looked over at Jordan. "Where's the panelboard?"

Jordan pointed toward the rear doors. "Door back there, marked 'Electrical Service.' To the right of the utility closet."

With a nod, Antonio toddled off, his tool belt dangling around his hips, giving him the stride of a sailor on a pitching deck.

Cam continued to envision how the place might look when it was ready for use for the foundation. Her architect had drawn up preliminary plans for the building, utilizing every bit of available space to its best advantage, including a greenhouse and vegetable garden out back to teach the children about responsibility, hard work, and healthy eating. Despite the vast nothingness, her brain filled in the blanks, and excitement grew. She hurried forward, turning in small circles as she pictured her vision come to life.

Her heels clacked on the floor in rapid succession, the sound thunderous in the cavernous space. Every noise seemed a slap at Jordan, who rolled along beside her, and she winced at how without meaning to, her very presence emphasized how far he'd fallen from the man she'd once known and loved. She should've worn jeans and sneakers, instead of a dress that showed off her legs and heels that emphasized every step she took. In trying to bolster her own ego, she'd managed to obliterate his. Talk about clueless. She glanced at him, and guilt constricted her ribcage.

"I'm sorry," she murmured.

He stopped in mid-roll to stare at her in confusion. "For what? You don't like the building?"

"No. I'm sorry I'm walking so fast."

To her surprise, he laughed. "Don't slow down on my account. And don't apologize either. It's not like I resent everyone around me because they still have two working legs."

"Well, you definitely resent me for *some*thing."

OH, HE HAD PLENTY OF reasons to resent Cameron Delgado. But here and now was not the time, nor the place, for that confrontation. Besides, she'd already managed to take him by surprise simply with the outfit she'd chosen to wear today. She looked like she was about to launch into a day of shopping, brunch, and a trip to the salon with her girlfriends, rather than inspect a dusty old office building.

All part of Cam's arsenal of quixotic charms. She had the ability to bring joy and color to the dullest activity with her choice of wardrobe, her talent for finding the humor in any situation, and her exuberant spirit. Yet, he also knew she saved her brightest fashions and snarkiest jokes for those instances when her ego was at its lowest.

Had he brought out that self-doubt in her? He didn't know how to feel about the possibility. Guilt mixed with a smidge of satisfaction. Toss in regret. Shake well and serve.

To change the subject, he pointed to the wall of windows that overlooked the busy street outside. "Plenty of space to display the little ones' artwork, and with the sheer number of passersby seeing those colorful handprint turkeys and lacy doily snowflakes, you'll draw a lot of attention. I'd suggest you put the foundation's name on every other window. No better advertising, in my opinion."

She nodded. "I agree." Looking down at her clasped hands, she murmured, "I should've called you back so I could come here sooner. From the time I first clapped eyes on this place, I sensed it was perfect for our needs. Being inside just confirms it."

Perfect. Yeah, he'd thought it was perfect for him, too—before Susan had swept the property out of his hands to gift wrap for Cam. Yet, as he watched her stroll around the site, he sensed how much she already loved the building and oddly, how much the building suited her.

Despite the commission he was about to earn, he still couldn't decide if doing business with her was good for him or the worst thing to happen since that game in Houston. Marcus had his opinion, of course, but Jordan had adopted an attitude of wait and see.

He faked a smile and prayed she didn't see through him. "Well, I'm glad you finally agreed to work with me. I agree. This place would be ideal for your Manhattan center. You know, despite all the water under the bridge between us, I've always believed in the foundation and the work it does."

Her lips tightened into a thin line. He knew that look. She was biting back something she knew she shouldn't say. Nice to see he could still get a rise out of her. Especially considering the water under their bridge was pretty toxic. He stifled the tide of bitterness before it could drown him.

Whatever struggle she fought behind those clamped lips, she won the battle to keep to herself. That was a new quality.

Instead, she asked, "How long have you been back in New York?"

"A little over a year." He stifled his disappointment that she'd learned how to monitor her words. Like her mother. What other of Laurel's off-putting habits had she acquired since he'd been gone? Besides ditching the man she claimed to love when he no longer served her purposes?

"And what made you go into commercial real estate?"

"My major in college was in construction management with a minor in business administration. With my football career over, it was good to have another occupation to fall back on." All facts she already knew, if she'd stopped to think about their shared history. But clearly, when she'd turned down his marriage proposal, she'd not only closed the door on their future, she'd also locked up their past in some dark, unvisited cellar. Now, they were virtual strangers to each other.

Still, if she could so callously toss him aside, he'd have to find a way to forget her as easily.

"That's smart," she said. "Bertie always tries to convince the younger players when they're being scouted to take their studies seriously. You're a prime example why that counsel is so crucial."

"How *is* Bertie these days?" He knew the answer, of course, but he and Bertie had both agreed Cam didn't need to find out about their conversation right away.

"The same." She shrugged and strolled ahead of him, her gaze flitting around the area as she scrutinized every corner. "How's Paris?"

He blinked at the non-sequitur. "The agent or the city?" She turned to glare at him over her shoulder, and it was his turn to shrug. "What? It's not like I've seen either one of them lately."

Cam stopped dead in her tracks and whirled, outrage stamped on her face. "She dumped you?"

"I wouldn't exactly put it that way. After all, for her, I'm only as good as my next contract. Once I snapped my spine on that field, our relationship became as useless as my legs."

"I'm sorry." She walked to the wall of windows. "That sucks."

"I'm not. It's business."

"There was more than business between you two."

He snorted. "You always hated Paris."

"Hmmph." She tossed her head and perched her bottom atop the rack of radiators, those mile-long legs of hers extended out across the floor, the toes of those ridiculous boots pointed up toward the ceiling. "I don't hate anyone. I didn't trust Paris. Turns out, I had good reason."

God, was she still carrying a grudge over his trade to Houston?

"Paris only did what I paid her to do: find me a place where I could use my talents for a team that needed me. Let's face it. With the Vanguard, I'd have always been second best. And with you, too."

"What's that supposed to mean?"

"Come off it, Cam. You didn't *need* me. You never did."

She pushed off the radiator and stood in front of him, her complexion pink with undisguised anger. "I may not have needed you, but I *loved* you. Not that you ever cared about love. If you had, you wouldn't have left me for the first better-looking, skinnier woman who made you hard."

"You think I left you for Paris?!" A bitter laugh escaped his mouth. "You are seriously delusional. I hired Paris for her business savvy, not for her looks. And yeah, she's skinny. So what?" Cam's sudden icy expression could freeze a bonfire, and he shook his head. "God, your mother's insecurities have screwed you up so bad. You've always been the most beautiful woman I know—inside and out. Any flaw, any bit of extra on you doesn't make you less loveable or less...*anything* in my eyes or in anyone else's, for that matter. But you never see that, do you?" She didn't answer, and her lips tightened again. "And one other thing, sweetheart. For what it's worth, before you and after you, *plenty* of women have made me hard."

"Ahem!" Antonio's sudden intrusion doused the fire crackling between them.

Great. Talk about perfect timing! Jordan reared back to regain some space and perspective. Whatever he and Cam once had, if anything, was long gone.

"Sorry to interrupt," Antonio said, "but I want to talk to Cam alone for a sec."

No problem. He could use the break from her anyway. "Sure. I'll go outside and wait for you there. Take as long as you need."

A hundred years wouldn't be long enough to get Cameron Delgado out of his system.

Chapter 6

Cam struggled to find ways to stay occupied for a full forty-eight hours before calling Jordan with her decision about the sale. Not that there was any doubt on her part. Reviewing the various reports from her bevy of attorneys and construction experts only left her more excited to begin the project. The site fit her needs to perfection: it came in under budget, sat in a good location, and left them plenty of room to grow. In the end, she'd simply needed time for her heart to catch up to what her head had known from the second she saw the place. There'd never been a doubt in her mind she'd acquire it, even if Jordan Fawcett was attached to it.

Still, Jordan needed to stew for a while. Leaving him dangling not only gave her the power position in their business deal, it gave him a taste of his own medicine. A few days in limbo only scratched the surface of the purgatory he'd sentenced her to.

"You should give him the green light in person," Bertie advised as they sat together in her office early one evening.

She studied him over the last page of financials. "Why? I never do that. Once the decision is made, it's a phone call at best."

He shuffled a packet of papers and placed them inside a folder. "Jordan's not your usual real estate agent." He tapped the cover. "You and he have personal business smeared all over this deal. Invite him to lunch. You need to sit down together, somewhere in public, alone, with no distractions and talk. *Really* talk."

Suspicion slithered across her shoulders. "What do you know that you're not telling me?"

His expression remained a bland mask. "Nothin'. I've just been thinking about the two of you and seeing things, not as your teammate in this game, but as your referee. Not taking sides. I'm observing. So, let's go to the videotape, as they say. What happened between you? He proposed; you turned him down. Meaning, your relationship had run its course. What'd you expect from him after that? Was he supposed to hang around here to carry your purse at social events?"

The sarcasm stung, and she jerked up her head to confront him with outrage. "Of course not! I wasn't ready for marriage. I may never be ready for marriage. That didn't mean I didn't still love him. I just…"

"You just wanted him to hang around on the off-chance you might change your mind someday. Give him a little leeway on his leash, but not enough where you can't yank him back when you need him at your beck and call."

She frowned. "That wasn't it at all. I wanted to take things slow." Of all people, *he* should understand her hesitancy to dive headfirst into a marriage. He'd never remarried after his divorce from her mother. "'I do' and 'happily ever after' have never been synonymous in my family. So, maybe I wasn't ready for an engagement ring and a fancy exchange of vows. Why couldn't we have started getting more serious by moving in together first?"

Bertie leaned forward in his chair and folded his arms atop the desk. "Did you ever tell Jordan that's what you wanted?"

Warmth flooded her face, and her throat tightened with regret. "He never gave me the chance. After I turned down his proposal, he immediately put up this wall between us. I knew he wouldn't listen to anything I said that night. I figured we'd talk the next day. Instead, he held a press conference with Paris to announce he'd signed that damn contract. He could've waited, given me a chance to explain, let me make a counteroffer. He didn't have to leave New York, leave the Vanguard, because I didn't want to get married."

"A counteroffer?" Bertie shook his head. "You talk about his proposal like it was a business deal. Love and business don't mix, sweetheart. Take it from me. Besides, I don't think the proposal and the trade were meant to happen in such quick succession. Or maybe he wanted you to come with him to Houston and figured a ring on your finger would get you to agree with less of a fight."

"He knows I'd never leave New York," she said with a snort. "Everyone and everything I love is here."

"Then I don't see how you can resent him for his choice."

She gripped the edges of her desk until her knuckles whitened. "He should have stayed loyal!"

Bertie's brow furrowed with lines of doubt. "To you? Or to the team? Look, Cam, forget about you and him for a second and think about where he was, professionally, at that precise moment. His career with the Vanguard was on the downhill side. You *know* that. He had, maybe, one good year left before we put Caceres into the starting position. Back then, the Privateers were a young team, and they needed a veteran to anchor their new, raw players. It was a perfect fit for Jordan and should have given him several more years with a major role on the field before he gracefully faded into retirement. Given the option, in his situation, I probably would have done the same thing."

She couldn't believe her ears. "But you're a Vanguard. Born and bred. Always."

"I'm a *football player*. So was Jordan. Yeah, it's nice to say you stayed with the same team from the day you were first drafted, but it rarely happens. I'm one of the very few lucky ones. I've lived the majority of my life as part of the Vanguard, and when I die, I plan to be buried on the fifty-yard line at the stadium so I can remain a part of the team into eternity."

Cam shook her head, smiling at his nonsense. "Don't say stuff like that, Bertie. You'll probably outlive us all."

"Probably." He gave her a careless shrug and a wicked grin. "I seem to be immortal. God knows, your mother did her best to kill me off while we were married. But you're missing my point. For ballplayers like me and Jordan, the game's in our blood. We *live* for it. Coaches change, managers change, and a team's needs change, season to season. None of that matters to us. All we care about is another day on the field, and we'll do whatever it takes to get it. Football beats the crap out of us, and like some obsessed lover, we keep running back for more. We'll ice our knees 'til they're numb, run laps at dawn, play in rain or snow or blazing heat. We shrug off the weather, tape up the bruises, and play through the pain. And yes, we'll even sign with a different team, if it gives us the chance for another day on the gridiron, one more game, one more quarter, one more play—until football has taken everything from us and we can't put on the cleats anymore. Sometimes, that happens 'cuz of a sudden death, like it did for your dad, and sometimes, it happens due to a serious injury, like with Jordan. Me? It'll probably be the arthritis that does me in eventually. But no matter how it comes or when, we know the odds going in. The end is always looming there in the distance. We know it, and we don't care. Nothing matters more than the game."

His voice was a harsh whisper by the time he finished his speech. Cam couldn't remember the last time she'd heard him talk about anything with so much passion.

She swallowed the reality sandwich he fed her with a curt nod. Facts were sometimes hard to accept, especially when they contradicted emotions. "Did Jordan ask for your opinion before...before he signed with the Privateers?"

"No. But if he had, I would've told him to go. Those kinds of opportunities don't come around every day."

Looking at the situation with candor, the way he asked her to, she had to admit Bertie's insight made sense. Still...

"None of that explains what happened at the hospital in Houston."

His lips tightened into a thin line. "No, it doesn't. Which is why you two need to clear the air. Something ugly reared up between you."

"Yeah." Bitterness stung the air. "Paris Redmond." Except she wasn't ugly. At least, not on the outside. Inside, though...

She grimaced.

Bertie shook his head. "I don't for one second believe Jordan was ever romantically involved with that piranha, but whether he was or wasn't doesn't change the fact that you and he lost your way somewhere, either right before or right after that proposal."

She shoved away from her desk and spun her chair toward the wall of windows looking out over the river. "I *told* you—"

"I'm not saying you did anything wrong, or that he did, either."

Whirling the chair around, she faced him again. "Then what *are* you saying?"

"Ask. Him. To. Lunch." He reiterated each syllable. "Sit across from one another. Talk. Tell him why you're angry at him, let him tell you why he's angry with you. Maybe you'll find you're *both* wrong."

She grabbed a pen off the desk and pointed the tip at him. "You know something you're not telling me. What is it?"

"All I know is that, for two people who claim to care so little about each other, you're both tiptoeing around your feelings like you're walking through a mine field."

"You talked to him?" She sat up straight in the chair. "When? Why?"

He waved a hand in dismissal. "Relax. We just talked football."

"Football?"

"Uh-huh."

Whenever Bertie wanted to talk about something serious without referring to the actual people involved, in her case it was usually about her mother, he'd fall back on talking football. He claimed couching something in football terms made it easier for him to remain objective. Thus, his need to remain objective when talking with Jordan could only mean one thing: they talked about her.

She leaned her chair back and feigned boredom, folding her arms over her chest and staring out the window again. Meanwhile, her pulse thundered behind her eardrums, and her lungs stuttered on the whole inhale-exhale routine. "What pressing football matter did he need to discuss with you?"

"He was reliving one of his past mistakes. Wanted my advice on how I would've handled the situation."

Outside her window, and many stories down, a ferry slipped across the silver surface of the water. She focused her attention on the grace and calmness of the simple white line left in the boat's wake until her breathing and heartbeat slowed to a normal rhythm. "Uh-huh. And how would you have handled it?"

"I told him I would've gone with a fumblerooski."

"A fumblerooski..."

The ferry glided on while she pondered what exactly he was trying to not tell her. Of course, she knew the play. She just had no idea how it referred to her and Jordan.

"Ask. Him. To. Lunch." When she didn't immediately react, Bertie balled up a blank sheet of paper and tossed it at her head.

She whirled then. "Hey!"

"What are you waiting for? Pick up the phone."

She picked up the phone.

CAM WAS ALREADY SEATED at a table when Jordan rolled inside The Blue Comet. Even among the thick crowd, he could still zero in on her whereabouts, as if they shared some voodoo radar. Her plum-colored blouse brought a tinge of honey to the razor-thinned ends of her hair where it brushed her collar, and a warm glow suffused her complexion. She took a delicate sip from a glass of white wine while her gaze stayed fixed on one of the televisions in the bar area, turned to, of course, a sports channel.

A wave of nostalgia washed over him as he stared at the brass-and-mahogany décor, the cozy saddle leather booths, and the horseshoe-shaped bar. The restaurant had been a favorite of theirs when they'd dated all those years ago, and entering now was like hurtling back in time.

With the maître d's attention focused on finding a suitable booth for the foursome ahead of him, Jordan allowed himself a minute or two to indulge in the past before he'd have to confront the present.

Cam kept her hair longer in those days, way past her shoulders, in gentle waves of spun gold that tickled his chest or caught the wind and tickled his nose. He, of course, wasn't sentenced to live in this cursed chair yet, and his standing height gave him a few inches over her, lending him the *appearance* of wielding the power in their relationship. Funny how he'd thought that so important in his youth, the whole mien of being in charge—especially with a dynamo like Cam.

Because, no matter his height, a person couldn't be in Cam's orbit and not realize she was a force of nature. Being tall didn't mean squat when you faced off against the whirlwind that made up the woman he once loved, a woman who could be frostier than February one minute, hotter than August the next. She was the hope of New Year's Eve, the love of Valentine's Day, the whimsy of St. Patrick's, the fireworks of the Fourth of July, the bounty of Thanksgiving, and the joy of Christmas. She was, in essence, the personification of every month of the calendar, all rolled up into one fantastic woman.

He'd thought she'd stay by his side forever, but he'd lost her to...

God knew what.

A football trade? Hard to imagine the love they once shared could be destroyed over something so petty.

"Mr. Fawcett?" The stern-faced maître d's prompt jerked him back to the present. "Ms. Delgado is waiting for you. I'll show you to her table."

Jordan waved off the man's stiff manner. "No need. I see her. Thanks." He maneuvered his chair around the waiting area, noting the other tables he passed seemed squished together more than should be comfortable.

The thought struck him and gave him pause. Cam had obviously asked the staff to give him more space, so as not to embarrass him in front of the lunchtime crowd while his wheels caught on furnishings as he made his way to the table—not their usual booth, which was another example of how she'd considered his weakness when planning this meeting. Probably because the last time they met, he'd reminded her of the challenges of maneuvering a chair in a crowded place.

He didn't know whether to be pleased at her insight or resentful that he needed that kind of insight. This, she could do: order furniture arranged to give him more room to move in a crowded restaurant. No doubt, she assumed the public would see and quietly remark to each other what a kind, thoughtful woman Cam Delgado was. But when the spotlight disappeared, and no one watched, the kind, thoughtful woman had left him floundering with no support whatsoever. He swallowed the sour memories and transformed the ensuing grimace into an uncomfortable smile.

"Hey, Cam," he greeted her with forced cheer. "It's been ages since I've been here. The old place still looks the same."

She started to slip out of her chair, but stopped halfway, as if realizing the bad optics of standing over him and having to stoop to meet his level. Resettling in her seat, she waited for him to situate himself opposite her and then extended her hand. "Jordan. Thanks so much for meeting me here today."

He wrapped his fingers around hers in a no-strings-attached clasp. "Happy to." He had no idea why she'd asked him to lunch, but he sensed it couldn't be good news. She must have decided against buying the Loughlin site after all. This was the kiss-off meeting, he could sense it in the air.

How would this turnabout affect him? Susan had been dancing in her office for days now. He doubted she'd take the news well.

So much for any possible fumblerooski to save *this* game.

Their waitress approached the table and asked if he wanted a drink. His first instinct was to order a scotch, but he quickly reconsidered and went with an iced tea instead. After she left, he pushed the menu to the side and leveled a steady gaze on Cam. "Now, that the drinks are out of the way, why don't you tell me why I'm here?"

She shook out her napkin and placed it on her lap. "Well..."

She wiggled in her seat, as if trying to get comfortable, which didn't bode well for what she was about to say. He steeled himself in his chair, his hands gripping the arm rests with white-knuckled strength.

"Normally, I'd just have Marty or Rose call you," she continued, "but I think I owe you more than a faceless conversation with one of the foundation's legal representatives. This news should come from me directly."

Here it comes, the gentle rejection...

He decided to head her off before she could dive into whatever speech she'd rehearsed to let him down easy.

"No problem. If you're not interested—"

"We want to buy the Loughlin site," she said at the same time.

On a series of rapid blinks, he relaxed. When he spoke again, his tone came out hushed and roughened with renewed hope. "I'm sorry. Did you just say you want to buy the place?"

She laughed. "Of course. You don't think I'd call you all the way down here just to say no, do you?"

"I'll be honest," he replied. "I wasn't sure what to think."

"Then I suppose this is a happy surprise for you." She tilted her wineglass toward him before taking another sip. "Would you like me to signal the waitress to come back so you can order something stronger to celebrate with?"

Well, that came out a little too condescending to Jordan's ears. Curling his lip, he waved away her offer. "I'm capable of flagging a person's attention when necessary on my own, thanks. But since I don't have the luxury of a private car and driver to chauffer me around Manhattan, I'll stick to the tea."

Her expression turned icy, and she set the glass down on the table with too much force, creating a *thunk* between them. "That was uncalled for."

"Why? It's the truth."

A truth she'd always hated to recognize. Because Cam wasn't just *football* royalty. Way before her dad had earned his first million with product endorsements, Cam's mother had come from a long line of New York society royalty.

"Why do you always have to throw my money in my face?" she demanded.

"Why do people climb Mount Everest? Because it's *there*, Cam."

Rumor said her great-great grandfather had invested in one or two of Cornelius Vanderbilt's ventures back in the nineteenth century, and the ensuing generations had managed to live off the interest from those investments ever since. Of course, each family member was also expected to increase the wealth with profits of their own, and not a single one of them had dared to disappoint.

Laurel Delgado Wallace Kiernan Moffit Ellison owned a string of designer jewelry stores and a major league baseball franchise (a not-too-subtle slap to Duke and Bertie, no doubt). Ironically, her never-ending cycle of marriage, divorce, marriage, divorce didn't come from some need to constantly marry up. Her individual net worth exceeded that of all of her husbands combined—and the tightest prenups made sure her money stayed her money. No, Laurel never married for cash or clout. She married for love—every single time. Unfortunately, she tended to fall *out* of love as quickly as she fell in. And when she fell out of love, the former object of her affections became a target for her disgust.

Before being allowed to take over the running of the Delgado Foundation, Cam had had to prove herself. Like her mother, she earned her first million while still a freshman in college. In Cam's case, she'd invested in green energy technology and financially backed a scientist who'd developed a hinge used in wind turbines around the world.

Unlike her mother, Cam didn't believe in love and romance and happily ever after. Too many stepfathers in too few years, followed by heated arguments and flaming departures, had permanently soured her on the idea of becoming a part of any semblance of a couple.

The bitterness returned, ready to overwhelm him, and he couldn't hold back the caustic words burning his tongue. "You try to pretend you're just like the rest of us, but you're not and you never were. Your money's this enormous wall that keeps you closed in, closed up, closed off. Occasionally, you'll let a peon like me into your world, but not forever. Never forever."

For a while, like some smitten teenager with his first crush, Jordan had thought the two of them stood a chance of making their relationship work—especially if he could have convinced her to move to Texas. Away from the drama her mother routinely inflicted, out of sight of the press, starting over somewhere new as a relative unknown, she could have lived the kind of life she always *claimed* she wanted.

Turned out, her whispered wishes to run away with him, give up the relentless spotlight, and focus on just the two of them had all been a lie. A sham she created to make him feel better about his unpolished, unmoneyed background.

Across from him now, her complexion paled, and all the celebratory air deflated from their surroundings. "As I recall," she retorted through gritted teeth, "*you* left *me*. I'm not the one who couldn't wait to sign a contract and move two thousand miles away."

Before he could respond, the waitress reappeared at his side with a tall glass of iced tea and a big smile. "All set to order?"

Jordan rolled back from the table. "On second thought, I can't stay," he replied. "Cam, I'll have our legal team send the contracts to your legal team. It would probably be for the best if you and I let them iron out the details without us."

Her lips tightened into a thin line. She took another sip of her wine and nodded. "I think you're right."

At her agreement, he turned and made his way back to the restaurant's main doors without another word. Next time they met, he should probably be armored for battle.

Chapter 7

Jordan was still fuming about Cam on Wednesday night when he and a group of friends met to watch the Yankees game at Marcus's apartment.

Marcus's wife, Theresa, greeted him at the door. She was tall and regal, dressed in a yolk-yellow jumpsuit that made her skin glow. A hammered gold neckpiece circled her throat and matching squares the size of dominoes decorated her earlobes. Theresa Haines was every inch a strong, Black woman with an ocean-sized heart and a laugh that could make you dance to its music.

He offered her the six-pack on his lap and, taking the cans, she bent to gather him close and give him a kiss on the cheek. Instantly, he was enveloped in the scent of gardenias.

"How are you, Jordie?"

Theresa was the only person in the world he allowed to use that juvenile nickname. "I'm good, Reese."

One ridiculous nickname deserved another.

"You sure? You seem a bit tense to me." She squeezed his shoulder. "Like you're carrying an awful lot of weight around here."

Luckily, she didn't wait to hear a denial. He'd hate to lie to her.

Releasing him, she pushed the door open wider with her hip then stepped back to give him room. "Come on in. Can I get you something to drink?" She held up the six-pack. "One of these, maybe?"

He shook his head. "Those are for you. Hard berry ciders. The ones we had at the vineyard out east last month."

"You found them?" Theresa looked at the cans, then shimmied on her toes. "Mmm. Mmm. Mmm. Please don't tell me you drove all the way out there again just to make me smile in the middle of the week."

"You'd be worth it, but no. Believe it or not, I found them in the supermarket near my place last week. Grabbed 'em and kept them chilled in my fridge until tonight."

She grabbed his hand, gave it a tight squeeze. "Well, thank you for thinking of me. That's why you're my favorite of all of Marcus's friends. The rest of those cretins drink the beer I go out to buy, eat the food I make, spill chips all over my floor, and then thank *him* for his hospitality. Like I'm just the maid or something."

"I'm sorry." He followed her as she sailed into the white-and-steel kitchen to the right of the front door.

"Hmmph! You don't have to apologize. You're not responsible for anybody but yourself." While sliding the six-pack into the stainless refrigerator, she asked again, "So, what can I get you to drink?"

"For now, I'll just take a water, thanks."

"You got it." She pulled out a bottle of water and shut the fridge door, leaning against it with her arms folded over her chest.

A loud exultation of "Yeah!" erupted from the living room area, and Jordan's head swerved in that direction.

"Here." She waited 'til he faced her again, then tossed the bottle at him. "Go on. Go hang out with your friends. I'll be fine by myself."

He would've offered to stay with her a little longer, but he was out of small talk topics. Not that she noticed. The minute he turned his back, he heard the distinctive sound of a pop top cracking open.

Yeah, she'll be fine.

He rolled his way into the living room, this area decorated in muted grays and purples, to join the cluster of men yelling at the television mounted on one wall.

"Hey, Jordan's here!" Marcus, the tallest of the group, announced.

Three of the five other men turned to give him a quick nod, the other two remaining engrossed in the game.

Jordan raised his hand in greeting while settling into a spot off to one side of the matching club chairs, where he could see the television clearly but not be in the way of the revelries. Past experience had taught him, after a few beers, these guys got clumsy. At last week's get-together at Don's place, Raymond had turned suddenly to grab a mozzarella stick, caught his size 12EEE foot in one of Jordan's wheels and sprawled into his lap, to the guffaws of all. Luckily, the beer bottle Ray held was empty, or Jordan would've wound up soaked and sticky, as well as embarrassed.

Marcus left the men standing around the screen and took the club chair beside him, one eye still on the game. "Hey. Glad you could make it." He perched on the cushion's edge, hands clasped, with fingers interlaced, balanced between his spread thighs. "How'd it go with Cameron yesterday?"

"It went fine."

His frustration must have shown on his face because Marcus muttered an expletive his sweet wife would never tolerate, if she'd been within earshot. Leaning forward, he whispered, "What the hell happened?"

"She asked me to lunch to tell me the foundation plans to buy the site. It all started out fine, and her news put me in a good mood, you know? But then she started rehashing our old history, who did what to whom and in what order. I wasn't in the mood, and I let her know it." He skipped the personal details of their conversation and glossed over his abrupt departure with a simple, "I didn't stick around after that."

"So you just walked out?"

With one eyebrow arched, Jordan gestured to himself seated in his chair. "Not exactly."

"Dude." Marcus shook his head. "You know what I mean. Was that smart? To leave her hanging like that? In public? I can't imagine she appreciated being dumped in the middle of a crowded restaurant. You couldn't just keep your mouth shut and let her vent for a few minutes? I mean, how does your temper tantrum yesterday affect the sale going forward?"

"A. There was no temper tantrum. I didn't make any kind of scene. I guarantee anybody watching would just assume I had to leave in a hurry but not because I was mad. B. It doesn't affect the deal at all. Before I left, we agreed to let the lawyers handle all the details until the closing."

"And then...?"

"And then we'll face each other across her big glossy board table in her conference room, but there'll be a dozen other people there with us. I'm sure we can remain civil in a crowd."

"Yeah, that worked so well for you two in a busy restaurant." With a grimace, Marcus leaned back to look up toward the heavens. "I shoulda known. I thought you said this was a win-win situation for us."

"It is!"

Marcus's head dropped level, and his eyes narrowed.

Jordan held up a hand to stem the brewing argument. "So, okay, we lost the ability to acquire the site ourselves, but the more I looked at it from her point of view, the more I realized it's much better for her purposes than ours anyway." Not the total truth, but if he said it aloud often enough, he silently hoped he'd come to believe it. "I've already got feelers out for a better space. And the commission I'll get from the Loughlin sale will put us in a stronger position to acquire something more suited for us."

"Yeah?" Marcus folded his arms over his chest. "Well, if this is such good news, why do you look like I just shot your dog when you talk about it?"

He uncapped the bottle of water and took a deep swig before replying, "Because dealing with Cameron Delgado is like facing a pack of rabid dogs. When she sinks her teeth into something, she refuses to let go. Years could pass by, and she'll still bring up crap that you've forgotten about—"

Chuck! A crack of the bat onscreen sent the rest of the group into raucous cheers, and both men veered their attention to the television where a player rounded the bases at a jog.

Distracted by the noise and the game, he blurted without thinking, "Cam has a way of getting under your skin until you wanna..." He cupped both hands, spread at least a foot apart, unsure what he could possibly say next. "She makes me crazy, that's all."

"Uh-oh," Theresa remarked as she maneuvered a bowl of chips around her husband's shoulders to place on the end table. "I'm pretty sure Marcus used to tell his mom the same thing about me."

Marcus snaked an arm around his wife's waist and pulled her into his lap. He pressed a kiss to her mouth and pulled away, smacking his lips. "Mmm...sweet. Raspberries?"

"Berry cider. Jordie brought them for me. They're deeee-licious." She kissed him again. "See?"

"Uh-huh." Craning his neck past Theresa, he mouthed to Jordan, "Alcohol content?"

Jordan shrugged. "Four? Five?"

"Nine," Theresa exclaimed.

Marcus's eyes rounded in surprise. "Nine?! How many ciders have you had, woman?"

"One." She held up an index finger and climbed out of her husband's lap to stand upright. "I'm not drunk. I'm sipping it slowly. I'm not a child, Marcus." Turning to Jordan, she added, "If you get tired of hanging here with these Neanderthals, join me in the kitchen. We'll talk about your Cameron."

His mood plummeted deeper. "She's *not* my Cameron."

Theresa winked. "Sure, Jordie. Not yet. But she *will* be."

"She was—once. I'll never make that mistake again."

"Really?" The lilt in Theresa's tone left no doubt he'd piqued her interest. "Oh, now, I want to know all the juicy details." She maneuvered behind him, gripped the handles of his chair and leaned over him, enveloping in her flowery fragrance again. "Marcus, I'm kidnapping your business partner. We've got stuff to talk about." Marcus glared at her, but she silenced any argument he might make on Jordan's behalf with the added comment, "Since my money's in this venture, too, I've got a right to know what we're up against."

"There's nothing to tell," he argued. "It was a long time ago."

"Uh-huh. As old as yesterday."

To Jordan's disappointment, Marcus got up from the chair. "Good luck," he muttered before rejoining his buddies around the television.

Jordan glanced up into Theresa's smug expression. "Was that last comment by your husband for you or for me?"

"Oh, you, honey. Definitely you." She cackled as she pushed him forward. "Your Cameron's ability to sink her teeth into something that interests her's got *nothing* on me. Let's go."

LATE FRIDAY MORNING, while he drowned in spreadsheets before an afternoon meeting with Susan, Rachel slipped into his office with a steaming cup of coffee. As she placed the mug on his desk with a *thunk*, she whispered. "Michaela wants to see you in her office. Now."

He glanced up, and she pressed a finger to her lips. What was with the cloak and dagger routine? "The blind wolf bays at the moon."

She blinked. "Huh? What are you talking about?"

Damned if he knew. "What are *you* talking about? I thought this was some kind of spy game you and Michaela cooked up with cryptic messages. I was just playing along."

"No spy game or cryptic messages." Cocking her head to one side and staring out the window, she seemed to reconsider for a minute. "Well, not really. But we do want to keep Susan out of the loop right now."

Now, *he* studied *her*. "Why?"

"You'll see. Come on. Leave the coffee. You'll want it when you come back."

Back from where? He still had no idea what was going on.

She straightened, hurried to the door, then waited. When he still didn't move, she jerked her head and widened her eyes. "Come *on*," she said through gritted teeth.

"What's the rush?"

"Oh, for God's sake." She stamped her foot. "Susan's out of the office, and her dragon lady assistant is in the lunchroom. Now's the best time for us to talk without anyone noticing."

"Noticing what?"

"That we're talking."

His head spun. How could he get off this ride? "Rachel, I—"

"Sssh! Talk on the way. Come on." She waved a hand with frenetic motion. "Hurry up."

"If we're in such a rush, why didn't Michaela come to me?"

"Because it's already up on her computer, and her office is the farthest away from the lunchroom."

Sure. That made as much sense as the rest of this conversation.

"Quit dawdling. Let's go!"

First Theresa, now Rachel. What had gotten into the women he knew? "All right, all right."

On a deep sigh, he followed Rachel out of the office and down the carpeted hallway to Michaela's office several doors away. As soon as he was inside, Rachel shut the door, locked it, and turned to peek through the side window out into the hall.

Oh, sure. No spy games here.

If he expected a saner response from Michaela, he was doomed to disappointment. She stood up from behind her desk and used both hands to wave him over, her voice no louder than a rustle. "C'mere, c'mere. Quick!"

"What is going on with you two?"

"We found you a building."

That got his attention. He pushed himself forward in double-time while Michaela swerved her monitor to give him a better view.

"It's in Hell's Kitchen. Corner unit, ground floor. Used to be a supermarket so it's got lots of open space. Eleven thousand square feet, plus a huge parking lot." She used a pencil to point out the open area of asphalt to the right of the building. "There's also a garage across the street for your more...*particular* clients."

Particular? No, more like private. Clients like he used to be: pro athletes, or maybe dancers, performers who might want to keep an injury under wraps from the press for as long as possible.

He stared at the photos on her monitor with a practiced eye. Good space. Plenty of windows. All on the ground floor, which gave him a comfort he hadn't felt at the other property. The Loughlin place had two stories with the offices upstairs, meaning, in case of any emergency, he could be stuck up there with no way out—a scenario he'd learned to keep in mind and prepare for in everything he did: choosing a job, a place to live, or even a hotel room.

"This looks terrific," he said. "Do you have specs?"

Michaela exchanged a panicked expression with Rachel, who rolled her hands and murmured, "Go on. Tell him." Before he could decipher the dread he'd noted in her eyes, she returned her attention to the narrow window.

"Yeah, please," Jordan said to both women. "'Tell him.'"

"It's not our listing."

Shit. "Then why show it to me?" Susan would have his head for going outside the agency.

"I know, I know," Michaela said. "But it's a great fit, don't you think?"

"Well, yes, it *would* be—if Susan was getting her piece of the action. But if she's cut out... " He mocked slicing a knife across his throat. "*Crrrrt!* We'll all wind up cut."

The ladies wouldn't look him in the eye, which raised the hackles on his nape. Clearly, there was something even scarier they weren't telling him.

On a hunch, he asked, "Who's the seller?"

Michaela's eager expression clouded. "Bella Richards."

His jaw dropped. "Are you insane?"

Bella Richards was originally one of the two Rs in HRR Corporate Realty, along with senior partner Lori Reynolds, but Bella left the firm in 2010, taking Susan's husband with her. Susan had never forgiven either of them for the betrayal—a betrayal made doubly worse when they opened their own corporate real estate office in midtown.

"Why don't we just shoot her in the heart? It would be less painful."

"Don't be a wuss, Jordan," Rachel retorted. "This is business. A site like this one doesn't come along every day. At least let us do some research. Susan doesn't have to know we're shopping. Not yet, anyway."

And if this deal went sideways, which was bound to happen, how quickly would these two push him under the bus? "Look, I appreciate you trying to help me with this but—"

"But nothing," Michaela interrupted. "Take a step back. Forget the ugly details. Just tell me the truth. If Susan was onboard, would you be interested in the property?"

He stared at the images again, interior and exterior, then turned his attention back to Michaela. "Probably. But you and I both know there's no way I can pursue it."

"Maybe, maybe not." Michaela shrugged. "I might have a way around that large, scary obstacle in the corner office. Give me a day or two. In the meantime, do you want to follow up on this? Set the wheels in motion? I can have Bella send me some specs, if you're interested."

He backed away from the desk, the computer, and the siren tempting him toward professional doom. "Not behind Susan's back, no."

Her lips twisted, displaying her disappointment. "Brown-noser."

Let her think what she wanted. While he did owe some loyalty to Susan for hiring him and giving him a chance, his reticence to pursue the building had more to do with empathy. The last thing he wanted to do was get in the middle of a romantic tragedy. He'd barely survived his own.

Chapter 8

At six o'clock, Val knocked on Cam's office door and poked her head inside. "Time to go."

Cam looked up from her computer and groaned. "Crap. Already?"

Dinner with Mom and Mr. Ellison waited on this Friday night. Just what she didn't need at the end of the week she'd endured. After that contentious lunch with Jordan on Tuesday, she'd come back to her office to discover her staff in an uproar. A burglary at their Atlanta location had resulted in the loss of thousands of dollars of school supplies, and with kids set to head back to classrooms within a week, Val, Casey, and several other employees were scrambling to replenish the coffers before Saturday's giveaway event was scheduled to occur.

Cam had joined in the melee, making phone calls and pulling strings to strong-arm office supply store managers into rushing shipments overnight so the staff down in Georgia could get the new supplies catalogued, stuffed into backpacks, or set up on displays for overextended parents to grab and check off their child's wish list. On Thursday, she and Val had flown down to help with the event and only arrived back home six hours ago. Now, she faced a critique session with her mom and Mom's latest husband *du jour*.

"Shoot me now." She scrubbed her fingernails through her hair, sending tingles across her scalp, barely registering on her sleep-deprived brain's Richter scale.

Val shrugged. "Sorry. Can't do that. You'll just have to muddle through like the rest of us. As for me..." She yawned wide enough for Cam to check her tonsils from the opposite end of the office. "I've got serious relaxation plans tonight. I'm trying a new entrée from my food subscription service, miso-glazed salmon with faro, followed by a hot date with my bathtub with a glass of chilled wine. Then, around nine or so, I'll put on my comfiest Vanguard nightshirt and settle in bed to watch the true crime network until I fall asleep. Don't

66

ask me why, but a little murder and mayhem knocks me out faster than sleeping pills."

God, what Cam wouldn't give for a night like that tonight! A few hours of solitude and then, blissful sleep. But, no. She had to suffer through several hours of stilted conversation and biting criticism, all while pushing around the steamed vegetables and mock meat on the family Flora Danica china. By the time she arrived home tonight, she'd be too wired and anxious to sleep so she'd pace the floors with her favorite comfort food, a bag of ranch-flavored tortilla chips. Her stomach burned in dread.

She glared at Val with envy. "Rub it in, why dontcha?"

"Get a move on," Val said with a cheeky grin. "The sooner you go, the sooner you can have it over with."

She pushed away from her desk and out of the chair before she could come up with some fake illness to back out of tonight's invitation.

Ninety minutes later, she sat in the formal dining room of her mother's home and stared at the broccoli and cauliflower—no sauce—decorating two sad-looking broiled chicken breasts and a colorful salad—no dressing—fit for a starving artist's canvas.

As she sipped icy water from her cut-crystal goblet, Cam suspected the minute she left, Mom would pull out a roast duck with cherry sauce, potatoes au gratin, asparagus with hollandaise and a baked Alaska for dessert. This pitiful offering was for *her* benefit, a silent rebuke to her curves and her weight and her size. Well, she could play this game, too. Maybe she'd have Larry stop at a fast food place on the way home and get her a burger and fries—mega sized. And ice cream for dessert.

"I hear you just got back from Atlanta," Mr. Ellison remarked from her right side.

She noted he toyed with his meager dinner, same as her. Probably couldn't wait to tear into that duck the minute she got into her car downstairs.

"Yup. Landed at JFK this afternoon, as a matter of fact. The local foundation down there ran into a snafu with the school supplies drive earlier this week. Val and I took care of it."

Her mother, seated across from her, studied her with razor-sharp scrutiny. "That explains why you look more drawn than usual."

She had to anchor her eyes to keep them from rolling to the back of her skull. "Wow," she said with no inflection. "Thanks."

Mom, of course, looked stunning. Her platinum blond hair was styled into a sleek bob, and she'd wrapped her slender figure in a salmon-colored, bonded crepe sheath with a split funnel neckline and cap sleeves. Around her throat, she displayed one of her own designs: a simple collar necklace of polished rose gold. The piece was deceptively understated. In retail stores, that pink metal bangle ran about three grand.

"Oh, you know what I mean," Mom retorted with one of those royal hand waves she used to dismiss anything Cam felt strongly about. "You should let Val handle the piddly details of the foundation. She's been with you...what? Three years now?"

"Almost five." Cam speared a stalk of broccoli and popped it into her mouth, mainly to keep from telling her mother to butt out of her business. The vegetable might as well be made of Play-Doh for all her taste buds could discern.

"There you go." Mom's head jerked in some kind of curt nod of approval. "I think it's time you started delegating more of the day-to-day running to Val. You could use the extra time you'd gain to seize your life and make something of it."

"My life is fine the way it is."

Mom blew air out her pursed lips. "*Fine*. Hair is fine. Sand is fine." She swept her fork back and forth in the air as if conducting the New York Philharmonic. "Life is supposed to be grand, adventurous, full of passion and romance!"

"No, thanks, Mom. You've lived enough of that kind of life for both of us." For a nation, in Cam's opinion, but she bit back the rest of her thought behind clamped lips.

"Maybe if you had more time on your hands, you could so something about those dark rings under your eyes." Mom's tone grew softer, edged with that false concern that always got Cam's back up. 'Find a new style for that mop on your head. You could join a gym. You've got such a beautiful face, sweetheart. If you'd just drop a few pounds, I'm sure you could find a man in no time."

Here we go, right to the heart of the matter. "I'm not looking for a man, Mother."

"Oh, come off it, Cameron. You don't want to spend your life alone." She made goo-goo eyes at Mr. Ellison. "Why, I'm grateful every day I ran into Andrew at that gallery opening two years ago. He's made my life infinitely richer."

Mr. Ellison picked up her mother's hand and kissed her fingertips. "I was the lucky one that day, darling."

Good thing the food was bland after all; that way, it wouldn't burn coming back up.

"I'm happy for you both. Honestly. But there's a big difference between living alone and being lonely. I *choose* to live alone, without a man I have to answer to if I work late or need to fly to Atlanta at a moment's notice, or if I decide I want to order a pizza for dinner because I don't feel like cooking."

Mom pointed with her fork. "That's your problem right there."

"What problem?" Oh, she knew what problem. After all these years, she'd have to be dense as a cinderblock to not understand Mom thought she had a problem with food. Every six-year-old who began an annual jaunt to fat camp each summer for over a decade understood exactly where Mom and/or Dad found them lacking. "I'm comfortable with my life the way it is. I have a lot of friends, a career I love—"

"And you show up to every social function without an escort," Mom interjected. "Or worse, with *Bertie*." She didn't even try to hide the disgust from her expression, and Cam's fury bubbled up inside her.

Cam picked up her knife and held it blade up, like a dagger she'd flash before slicing an enemy's throat, and threatened through gritted teeth, "Don't say one nasty thing about Bertie or so help me, I'll—"

"Darling, please." This time, Mr. Ellison cut into the danger zone. "Let's not talk about this right now. Besides, I think Cameron's independence is admirable and courageous. It may seem strange to you, but it's a generational thing. Young men and women of today tend to find our social strictures archaic and... dare I say?" He shot an amused glance toward Cam. "...sexist."

Loosening her grip on the knife handle, Cam nodded in approval. Maybe this latest heartthrob still had a working brain cell or two not rendered stupid by Mom's stunning beauty and constant demands for inane fawning.

As if he knew her thoughts, he gave Cam a saucy wink. "Let your daughter be, darling. She seems to be doing fi—" He must have recalled her mother's reaction to the first use of the word, fine, because he quickly changed to, "*well* on her own."

Mom reached out a hand to clutch at Cam's wrist. "I just want you to be happy, Cameron. Settled. With someone who'll love you unconditionally."

Cam's taut nerves snapped. "Since when does settled mean loved unconditionally, Mom? You've been settled...what? Five times already? Were you always happy? Did you love Bertie unconditionally? Or Dad? Or Mr. Moffit? Will you love Mr. Ellison here unconditionally when he forgets to pick up his socks once too often or orders the wrong flowers on Valentine's Day?"

Mom's face colored the exact hue of her dress, and her lips clamped into a tight line, creasing lines in her forehead.

Crap. She'd gone too far. "I'm sorry," she muttered and pushed away from the table. "I should go. I'm sorry."

"No, Cam, stay," Mr. Ellison said.

Her mother remained stiff and silent.

Cam shook her head. "I think I've overstayed my welcome tonight." She faced her mother. "I'm sorry," she said again.

It wouldn't matter if she hired a plane to skywrite the words. Mom would only forgive on her own terms, no matter what the offender's relationship. Wasn't that the point Cam had just driven home?

She stood, placing her napkin beside her barely-touched plate. "Thanks for dinner."

And so went the crummy end to the crummiest week she'd endured in years.

BACK AT HER APARTMENT, her trusty bag of tortilla chips ignored on the sofa table, Cam paced figure eights in her floor and tried to come up with someone to talk to. Because despite what she'd boasted to her mother, Cam had very few friends to confide in.

Oh, she had lots of pals: guys she'd call to shoot a few games of pool down at Brady's Place, former classmates she'd join for girls' weekends or social brunches, and coworkers who were always up for a few drinks at happy hour. Funtime people.

But someone she could call on a Friday night to talk her off the ledge after a contentious get-together with her mother? That was usually Bertie's job. And tonight, he wasn't answering her texts.

Staring out the window at the traffic on the West Side Highway hundreds of feet below her, she scanned her mental contact list for someone, *anyone*, who'd be available, patient, empathetic, and judicious without being judgmental.

One name came to mind. She hated the idea she might be interrupting something important, or just intruding on what should have been a stress-free, peaceful evening. Besides, she'd never called before—not socially, anyway. That alone could make things awkward. Still...

Why not reach out and try? They were friends. Weren't they? Only one way to find out. On a deep inhale for courage, she picked up her cell and hit the preset on her favorite contacts screen. Huh.

Funny.

Favorite.

I bet there are very few of my contacts that have me listed as a favorite.

No. Don't go there. You're feeling sorry enough for yourself without the mental self-flagellation.

Lucky for Cam, this particular favorite answered on the second ring. "Hello?"

"Val? Umm... hi. It's Cam."

"Cam. Hi." Her reply was hesitant, which told Cam she *was* intruding. Crap. "Did... something happen... at the office?"

A guilty flush warmed her cheeks and tightened her throat. Pathetic that in all the years they'd known each other, Cam had never once called Val if the situation wasn't work-related. Until tonight. Val would have every right to blow her off and tell her to kiss off. Cam swallowed hard and plowed ahead, expecting nothing, yet hoping for more kindness than she'd ever bestowed.

"No," she said, her tone rough with dread. "I'm sorry to bother you. I was... umm... just wondering..." God, why was this so hard? *Just spit it out, idiot!* "Umm... how was your dinner?"

"Awful," Val replied. "The company tells you these meals are foolproof, you know? Well, that may be, but they sure aren't Val-proof. I put it in the oven and then I fell asleep on the couch. Next thing I know, the smoke alarm's going off, and I've got a charcoal briquette for dinner. Did you ever burn fish? It took a whole can of air neutralizer and six window fans to get rid of the stink."

Cam dug up a smile of camaraderie. Cooking was not something she'd ever mastered, either. "Well, I give you props for trying. I don't suppose you'd be interested in splitting a pizza with me, would you? My treat."

Did she imagine the slight hesitation on the other end? Maybe. Either way, she deserved it, she supposed.

"Only if you're willing to come here. I'm already in my pajamas. I think our trip took more out of me than I realized."

Yeah. She felt much the same way. "I can do that."

"Can you come here in your jammies?" Val added. "'Cuz, if you show up all glammed up in a pretty pink dress and heels, I'm taking the pizza and slamming the door on you."

Actually, that sounded fun—a pajama party kinda thing. Stress-free, hair-down, and no boys allowed. "I can do that."

"And no work talk! It's Friday night, we've had a grueling week, and I want the next two and a half days for vegging out."

"Not a problem."

"You'll have to come out by car. I'm in Nassau County. And you definitely don't want to jump on a crowded train on a Friday night in the summer. Especially if you're in some shortie pajamas."

"True." She'd have to call the service. See who was available tonight. But Val was right. She did not want to risk the pressing bodies on the Long Island Railroad trains. "Okay. Anything else?"

"Yeah. I like pineapple on my pizza. If that's a deal-breaker, now's the time to speak up."

She stifled her distaste; she needed this tonight. If that meant pineapple, so be it. "No deal-breakers. I'll be there in about an hour."

"Grab yourself some wine for the ride. I'm gonna have a helluva head start on you by then."

Cam grinned. "I'll bring more."

Sure enough, an hour later, she climbed up onto the wraparound porch of a blue, two-story colonial situated on a busy side street off the parkway, a bottle of wine (minus a glass or two) in one hand and a box containing a Hawaiian pizza in the other. She felt only slightly ridiculous wearing her neon yellow pajamas dotted with gray cats playing with pink balls of yarn and a pair of scuffed white Converse sneakers. Cam didn't have a free hand, but the front door opened from the inside before she could juggle her burden.

Thank God, Val must have been keeping an eye out for her. "Hey," she said as she slapped the latch to open the storm door. "Come on in."

Her assistant wore a knee-length, faded blue nightshirt with the maroon Vanguard logo above the words, "2010 National Champions."

Cam gave a curt nod. "Cool shirt."

"Thanks. Work perk." She led the way past the cozy, traditional-style living room with a cream-colored stone fireplace and furniture full of soft, curved edges in muted textile patterns of beige and gold. Giving Cam a wink over her shoulder, she added, "I can get you one of these nightshirts, if you want. I've got a friend on the inside."

"Yeah, totally not necessary. I have my own inside man with the team." Cam glanced at the bookshelf near the wall separating the living room from a small formal dining room. She noted the assortment of paperbacks, mostly romance, but a few mystery and suspense titles mixed in, so totally Val. If they weren't boss and assistant, she and Val could be close friends. They seemed to share a lot of the same interests.

Well, that was what she came here for, right? To disconnect from work and be with a friend?

Val stopped short at the doorway to the kitchen, and Cam, still focused on the bookshelf, walked pizza-box-first into Val's chest. Both women gasped. The box collapsed like an accordion, and only Val's quick reflexes caught it before the pizza fell out and landed on the carpet.

With the box cradled between them, Val looked up at Cam, brows knitted. "Crap. I'm sorry. I guess I'm not used to having 'The Boss Lady' in my house."

Desperately trying to balance her hold on the box and the bottle of wine, Cam shot her gaze over Val's shoulder toward the interior of the kitchen. "Can we put this stuff down and then talk?"

"Sure. I mean, I guess. I mean you're the boss."

The confused hesitation Val displayed almost had Cam second-guessing this decision. Almost. But she'd come to some tough conclusions in the last hour or two, and a moment's nervousness on Val's part wouldn't shake her.

"Tonight, don't think of me as the boss, okay? Please?" After placing the pizza on the set table in the middle of the eat-in kitchen, Cam held up the wine bottle. "Got a glass for this?"

"Yeah, sure." Val sidestepped the table and stood on tiptoe to reach a cabinet above the built-in microwave.

Crap, the last thing Cam wanted right now was a fuss. She wanted tonight to be easygoing, lazy and just plain fun. "Oh, don't go out of your way," Cam insisted. "Please. Anything is fine."

"No, don't worry. I got it." She retrieved a cut-glass water goblet from inside, then twisted to hold it out toward Cam. "This okay?"

Though she would've preferred something smaller and simpler, she sensed her new friend was trying to make a good impression. She wouldn't make her even more anxious.

"It's perfect. Thanks." She took the glass, filled it about halfway then passed the bottle to Val, who waved her off.

"I'm good, thanks."

They settled at the table, and Cam flipped the lid to the pizza box, surveying the damage with a critical eye. "Minor casualties. A few of the slices on one side are a little crushed. We'll save those for after we've had more wine."

"Umm... I can eat those. You don't need to have a bad slice—"

"Val." Cam's patience frayed at the ends. "Stop. Relax. Have another glass of wine. You're still going to have a job on Monday, no matter what happens tonight. I repeat. I'm not here as your boss. I'm here because..." She took a deep breath and sat at the table in the window nook. "Well, because I need a friend."

Val's eyes widened. "And you called me?"

Cam sipped her wine before answering. "Don't look so surprised. You're one of the most level-headed people I know. You're honest, discreet, and trustworthy. I value your opinion—"

"You do?" Cam's exasperation must have shown on her face because Val added, "I'm sorry. This is just... weird, you know? I mean, in all the years I've worked for you, you've never popped over for pizza and wine before. I don't know how to handle this."

Neither did she, to be honest. So, maybe that was the way to move forward: by being honest.

"Remember how you talked to me on the phone a little while ago? When you gave me your list of conditions if I planned to come over?"

Her cheeks flushed pink, and she shrugged. "Well, yeah, but that's when I thought there wasn't a snowball's chance in hell you'd come here."

Shoot. She hadn't considered the possibility Val only said yes because she feared she might lose her job or be punished in some way for saying no.

Her tone roughened to an embarrassed whisper. "Did you not want me here tonight, Val? Be honest. I swear, this has nothing to do with your job. The thing is..." God, how could she explain where her head was at? She took a deep breath and plowed on. "The thing is, I just left my mother's house and, as usual, it didn't go well. I mean, you know how she gets me amped up. And I really needed someone to talk to." Her throat tightened enough to limit her speech and, blinking back tears, she gulped some wine to loosen her tongue and drown her pride. "I realized I needed a friend, a confidante, and I don't have too many of those. But of all the women I know, you're the one I trust most. You're the one I'd like to be my friend. But I should've realized you were just being polite. I'm sorry for disturbing you."

She got to her feet, and Val rushed closer, hands outstretched. "No, no. Don't go. I get it. I do. I admit, you kinda had me wondering, but I understand now. When I'm down, I at least have my mom to talk to, and if my mom annoys me, I can talk to my sister. But when *your* mom is the problem, you don't have a sister or anybody else to confide in." As if realizing how pathetic that sounded, she winced. "I keep shoving my foot in my mouth when I should be eating pizza instead. You, too. Come on. Sit down. Let's eat and talk and have some fun." She reached into the box and pulled out a slice of pizza, then waved it under Cam's nose. "Mmmm... doesn't this smell good?"

"Yeah, it does." Relaxed at last, Cam smiled and sat down again.

Chapter 9

Two hours later, Val was out cold on the couch and Cam was too wired to concentrate on the espionage thriller playing on the television in Val's cozy living room. Despite Val's protests to the contrary, it was clear to Cam she'd intruded on what would've been a quiet evening of relaxation and decompression. Not the best way to initiate a friendship.

Since she'd already worn out her welcome, she wouldn't intrude on Val's solitude any longer. She wandered into the kitchen, searching for something to use to leave a note. After digging through several cabinet drawers, she finally came across a blank note pad with the foundation's logo across the top.

Cam smirked and glanced at the snoring Val. "Another work perk?"

Not that she minded. As long as Val didn't graduate to taking home printers and computers, the occasional pilfered notepad wasn't going to hurt anyone.

Another dive into the flotsam and jetsam of batteries, rubber bands, chip clips, and takeout packets in the kitchen drawer, and she found a pen. She wrote a brief note:

Val,

I'm so sorry to have hijacked your evening. Take Monday off and rejuvenate. When you wake up tomorrow, call Zehra at my spa for an appointment for you. I'm authorizing her to give you a full treatment. You've earned it! Then come back to work on Tuesday, refreshed and ready to work.

See you then.

Cam

She left the note tacked on the refrigerator using a magnet of a grumpy-faced Garfield holding a coffee cup with a curlicue of steam. Beneath the cartoon cat's feet, a box stated "I don't do mornings."

Yeah, she imagined Val would have a doozy of a hangover tomorrow, regardless of what hour she finally opened her eyes.

Unfortunately, for her, the night still loomed, lonely and long. She checked her phone. Just past nine o'clock. Great. Nothing to look forward to but the recriminations inside her head when she went home. Outside, the summer air was thick with humidity and sparks of lightning illuminated the dark clouds one at a time. A storm approached. At the curb, the limousine waited, and she opened the door to climb into the back seat. A destination came to mind, lighting up the clouds of her brain.

"Everything okay, Ms. Delgado?" the driver asked, placing the book he'd been reading on the passenger seat. "I wasn't expecting you to return so fast."

"Yes, Danny, thanks. Val's exhausted. But I'm not ready to go home just yet. Let's stop over at Brady's Place, okay?" She rolled her shoulders and stretched her legs out. "I could use a game or two."

"Sure thing."

As she settled against the black leather and tilted her head back, her driver pulled the car from the curb at Val's home, aimed for a return to the city.

A short time later, she strode inside Brady's Place, the official pub of the Vanguard teammates since 1967. The front room was empty, except for the heavy-set, curly-haired man who stood behind the bar, reading a magazine spread out across the polished top. Above him, a television aired a baseball game.

He glanced up at her entrance and straightened to full height. "Hey, Cam. How've you been?"

The sharp crack of a cue against a rack of balls, followed by an assortment of masculine laughter, told her there were at least a few patrons in the back. Good. She needed the distraction if she had any hope of sleeping tonight. Forcing a smile through her bouncing anxiety, she replied, "Good, Sal. You?"

"Can't complain." He pulled the bar towel off his shoulder and wiped his hands. "What can I get you?"

She slid into a booth near the rear of the room. "I need a vodka club with lime."

"Uh-oh," a too-familiar voice said from the doorway leading to the pool hall area, causing Cam to stiffen in her cushy seat. "Vodka lime can only mean another spat with Mom."

Cam's eyes shot open, and she veered in her seat to see the last man she'd expected to run into in this place. "Jordan. What are you doing here?"

"Waiting for a friend who's delayed on the subway. Are those... " His gaze raked her from throat to feet. "...pajamas?"

She clutched her collar and swiveled to hide her legs beneath the booth table again. Too late, of course. He'd already seen the ridiculous cats and yarn on the sunny yellow fabric she wore. Good thing she hadn't added bunny slippers to the ensemble. A heated blush rushed into her cheeks. "Yeah... umm... long story."

"Gotcha." On a quick nod, he rolled closer, stopping when he reached the edge of her table, his brow furrowed in question. "May I?"

She gave him the go-ahead with a wave of her hand. "Of course."

Despite the way their last meeting ended, she actually welcomed his intrusion. Jordan always had a soothing way when it came to her blowups with her mother. And since Bertie still wasn't answering her calls, she'd seize the opportunity to smooth over the rough edges they'd encountered at their last exchange.

"Thanks. I need a place to hide right now." Jerking his head toward the doorway to the back room, he replied, "I just lost three games in a row to Luis Blades."

An amused snort escaped her lips. "Yeah, Luis loves new bait in here. Did he tell you he used to make a living as a pool shark? Because he's supposed to, but he sometimes conveniently 'forgets.'" She curled her fingers around the last word. "The regulars tend to avoid playing him—unless he's handicapped with a less stellar partner—so when someone new comes in, the shark smells blood in the water and tries to take a bite."

Jordan frowned. "He made a living...?"

The stricken look in his eyes suggested he'd been bitten. Cam's impatience rose. "You didn't play for money, did you?"

His cheeks flushed. "He took me for fifty bucks."

"Oh, for God's sake." She slid to the edge of the booth and came up short due to the proximity of his wheels. "Back up a little, wouldja?"

"Let it go, Cam. I can afford the loss."

"That's not the point. Now, skootch."

He backed up a few feet, and she strode to the back room with purpose. "Luis!"

A half-dozen men stood around the pool table, some laughing, others sipping from beer bottles.

Her target had his back to the doorway, but turned at her shout. "Hey, Cam! How's it going? You here for another humiliating loss?"

"No. I'm here to make sure you give Jordan back his money."

"What are you, his mommy?" Guffaws erupted around them, but she planted her fists on her hips and waited, tight-lipped, until Luis stamped his cue stick on the scarred wooden floor. "Aw, c'mon! It's fifty bucks. Big shot can afford it."

"It's illegal, and you know it."

He shrugged. "Who's gonna tell?" His comrades continued laughing, adding choruses of "Yeah," and "You tell her," and "No snitching."

The tension of the last few hours got the best of her, and she snatched the pool stick out of his hand.

Her voice increased in volume and fury with every syllable. "You wanna get this place shut down? Now, give him back his money. You play for bragging rights, nothing more. Got it?"

The last two words came out in a shout loud enough to shake the walls. All five men facing her stood slack-jawed at her outburst. Reason returned, along with a heavy dose of embarrassment.

"Sorry," she said in a much softer tone. She passed the pool stick back to Luis. "Just pay him back. Okay?"

Without waiting for a reply or viewing the reactions to her tantrum, she turned, skittered past Jordan in his wheelchair, and returned to her booth then buried her face behind her hands. Damn, damn, damn! She should cut her losses, go home, dive head-first into that bag of tortilla chips that had been whispering come-hithers to her since before she arrived at her mother's home earlier this evening and hide from the world until Doomsday.

"Care to talk about it?" Jordan whispered.

She spread her fingers wide enough to see him through the gaps and found him in the exact place he'd been before she'd lost her mind in the back room. After that blowup back there with Luis, coming on the heels of their previous disastrous meeting, she would've bet her last pair of clean underwear he'd stay far the hell away from her right now.

Why was he suddenly being so nice to her?

At that moment, Sal appeared with her drink, placed a napkin on the table and set the glass on top. "Kitchen's still open if you want something to eat." He looked at Jordan. "Can I get you anything?"

"A ginger ale would be great, thanks."

"No sweat. You want anything to eat with that?"

Jordan waved a hand in dismissal. "I'm good. Cam?"

"No thanks." On a sigh, Cam dropped her hands to the table and shook her head. "I had a slice or two of pineapple pizza an hour ago."

Jordan cocked his head at her. "Pineapple? Since when do you indulge in that sacrilege?"

"Since a friend insisted," she retorted, then sighed at her short fuse. "Sorry. I shouldn't have snapped. The pie wasn't awful, but it's definitely not something I'd choose to eat on my own."

She knew why she'd snapped. She found it disheartening he still knew her habits so well, particularly since he'd made it plain he wanted nothing more to do with her, except business. She couldn't compete with a beauty like Paris Redmond, who could be both a romantic interest and a business partner. What was the line from that old movie? *I have a head for business and a bod for sin.*

Cam had the brains, but her figure was all "too" for sin, especially when compared to the wives and girlfriends of Vanguard players. Too tall, too big, too buxom, too... *too.*

It didn't matter that all her doctors assured her she was healthy and her weight wasn't an issue. As long as she couldn't fit into a size two like Mom, she'd never be good enough in some people's eyes. Certainly, not for her mother—and, apparently, compared to Paris Redmond, not for Jordan, either.

Maybe she should shake things up a bit in her routine. Try that new diet Val told her about earlier. Eat only foods that started with the letter L.

Oh, who was she kidding? Years of fasting and gallons of lemon water with cayenne pepper hadn't changed her shape or frame. She was built like her father, like her father's sister, and like the generations of Delgados who'd come before them both. Good peasant stock, Bertie called it. Able to withstand life's tragedies and remain on her feet. Capable of inordinate amounts of love.

In the good old days, before Houston came calling, she'd never doubted Jordan loved all of her, including her size. But after that incident in the hospital and the smug smile on Paris's face, the insecurities flooded in, pushed along on her mother's continuous tides of criticism. Bertie was the one man to pull her up out of her self-pity, to insist she value herself. And she did—or at least, she had. Until Jordan returned, along with all those old insecurities.

"What'd your mother say this time?"

Jordan's question brought her out of her musings. "If this is because I got your money back," she muttered, "you don't have to entertain me. Go on back and play with your friends."

"*You're* my friend."

She stared up at the tongue-and-groove ceiling. Clearly, the universe wasn't through messing with her this week. Because the last thing she would assume Jordan considered her was a "friend." Not after Tuesday. Or the hospital. Or the trade to Houston.

"I only met those guys tonight," he added. "And since none of them bothered to tell me the rules about Luis's shenanigans, I think calling them 'friends' goes too far. Somehow, I think they'll be fine without me. So what'd your mother say this time?"

Cam didn't attempt to fake a denial. "It's not what she said. It's what I said in response." She took a deep sip of her cocktail and let the alcohol tickle her taste buds before swallowing. "I don't know how I could be so stupid. I was jet-lagged. I was hungry. And she was serving this stupid dry chicken breast and tasteless vegetables, and she's all dolled up in a slinky dress and..." God, she had to stop rerunning it in her head like instant replay—forward and reverse and forward and reverse. "...she just got to me tonight."

"Why? What'd she say?" he pressed.

Another sip, another zing on her tongue. "That's the stupid part. She didn't say anything I haven't heard a thousand times before. I look tired. Of course, I look tired! I'd just put in a fourteen-hour day. I should fix my hair. Because that's the most important thing on my mind right now. If I hit the gym more often, maybe I could catch a man."

Cam swirled the contents of her glass, allowing the ice cubes to clink against each other. She didn't want to reveal all this to him. She wanted Bertie. Bertie, who never abandoned her when she didn't react the way he'd anticipated. Bertie, who loved her unconditionally—the way she once thought Jordan loved her. Tears stung her eyes, but she blinked them back.

"The thing is," she continued, still staring at the clear liquid and little slice of green spinning in her glass, "Mom always says the same stuff. She just wants what's best for me. She worries about me. She wants to see me settled with someone who loves me *unconditionally*. Normally, I shrug it off, but tonight..."

As the centrifugal force slowed, she placed her glass back on the cocktail nap-kin. "Tonight, I went off on her."

Jordan folded his arms on the table and leaned closer. "What'd you do?"

"I didn't *do* anything, not physically. When she started the unconditional love crap, I pointed out to her that, with her marriage record, she's a lousy ex-ample of loving anybody unconditionally."

He gave her a curt nod, but his expression remained inscrutable. "Good point. How'd she react to that?"

"She got all stiff and frowny-faced, and she shut down. Like her whole body became one big open wound. I swear to God, she got so hurt so fast, she was practically bleeding out her eyelids." The memory of her mother's reaction sent a chill down her spine, and she hugged herself to ward off a round of shivers. "She can say whatever she wants to me, and I've gotta take it because she's my mother. But I snap back at her *just once*, and I'm the world's worst daughter for hurting her feelings. I couldn't handle her expression, or the iciness in the room. So I said I was sorry, got up, and left."

He waited a beat, saying nothing, staring at her, until she glared back at him. He blinked first. "You mean, that's it?"

She slapped a hand on the table top. "Yes, 'that's it.' What'd you expect? That I set fire to the plates or something?"

"No, I'm just wondering why you're so upset over it, that's all. Did she at least acknowledge your apology?"

"No."

His lips twisted in a smirk of distaste. "Not surprising. Don't tell me you expected her to."

She hugged herself even tighter. "No."

"So, then, what's the problem? You told her a truth she needed to hear. Quite frankly, you probably should have said something to her at least two hus-bands ago."

"You didn't see her reaction." Her throat dried on the last word, and she grabbed her drink to take a deep swig.

"She'll get over it. I know her. And I know you. She loves to play the drama card, and you swallow your impatience every time she puts on a performance, instead of putting her in her place." He narrowed his eyes and pointed a finger at her. "Too much of Bertie's influence there."

"Don't *you* start." She was not about to listen to someone else try to malign her one and only support system.

Sal returned with a tall glass of ginger ale and another napkin. "Everything okay, Cam?" His eyes narrowed in suspicion toward Jordan.

She waved him off. "Everything's fine."

"Hey, Cam!" Luis called out from behind her. "Feel like playing a game? The guys are tired of getting their butts kicked."

Yes. She craved the release of cracking a few balls. The innuendo wasn't lost on her, and she hid her smirk behind her glass then drained the contents. She glanced at Jordan. "You wanna play doubles? Between us, we can take him. It'll give us both back a little ego tonight."

He grinned. "I like the way you think."

She got to her feet and proclaimed, "Rotation game with partners. Me and Jordan." Pointing between the two of them, she skooched out of the booth to stand beside him.

"You're on." Luis clapped his hands and offered a toothy smile full of confidence and bravado. "Me and Kenny against you two. Let's do it."

JORDAN GLANCED AT HIS watch and mentally tried to push time ahead. Marcus should have been here by now. If he'd had the brains he was born with, he would have turned down Cam's offer to team up to take down Luis and headed home. At least, he should have asked her where she'd been between dinner with her mom at six and her sudden appearance at Brady's Place almost four hours later. The friend she'd shared a pizza with had also shared some kind of alcohol with her, since that one vodka lime had clearly put her over the top. The classic rock music blaring from the overhead speakers set her into dancing mode, swishing her hips, singing along, her fingers caressing her pool cue in...provocative ways.

While the idea of regaining his dignity on the pool table had seemed like a good one at the time, playing with Cam came with a unique set of challenges he hadn't considered. Every time she bent over the pool table, her curvy butt was directly in his line of sight. Her fun-loving, competitive spirit woke up and took center stage. Every time she pocketed a ball, she'd rush back to his side and wrap her arms around his shoulders to celebrate. When she missed a shot or their opponents pocketed one of their balls, she'd grab his hand and squeezed his fingers as if to reassure him.

Currently, the teams were tied, with each pair having pocketed three of the opponents' balls. He and Cam were the stripes, tasked with sinking balls numbered nine through fifteen. Meanwhile, Luis and Kenny had to sink solids one through seven. First team to sink all their balls, in numerical order, followed by the eight ball, won.

Cam took her shot. *Crack*! *Click.Click.Click.* The cue ball slammed into several balls before hitting the purple twelve, sending it directly toward the corner pocket—where it stopped half an inch from falling.

"Ohhhh! Too bad, sunshine. That's tough luck. For you." Luis snickered, and Kenny followed suit.

Cam's expression remained placid as she gave a nod, turning the table over to Kenny.

He strode around the table, surveying the four ball from a dozen different angles, crouching here, leaning there, and frowning all the while. In moving the twelve ball closer, Cam had also caused a chain reaction that put the eight ball in a vulnerable position with the four.

While Kenny played his mind voodoo over the felt table and Luis looked on with some concern, Cam came to stand beside Jordan, and clapped in an up and down motion, as if smacking dust off her hands. "That should take some of the air out of those two windbags. Kenny's bank shot is his weakest move."

Having her so close to him played havoc with his memories. At one time, he'd been crazy in love with her. He'd loved her curves, her softness, her huge appetite for life—and love. In the bedroom, in the boardroom, in every place and every way, Cam gave and took with equal measure, but always in generous amounts.

Resentment simmered beneath his surface. After his injury on the field, he'd yearned for her to be there with him. The Cam he thought he knew would have dropped everything to stay by his side through the surgeries and the rehab and the endless hours of doubt and despair. Too bad the Cam he thought he knew had turned out to be a fantasy.

Yet, tonight, in Brady's Place, he saw a few embers of the old Cam: the silly pajamas she wore with the same dignity she'd display while dressed in a designer evening gown or a pair of jeans and a sweatshirt, her quick rush to his defense when she'd learned Luis had fleeced him, her vulnerability when she talked about dinner at her mother's, the confidence she oozed while playing this game, the music, her slightly off-tone singing, the dancing. All of it, pure Cam.

Don't fall for it, stupid. Not again.

He had to remind himself that the real Cam was the one who'd cut him from her life and never looked back. This charming woman beside him would only last until the ink dried on the sale contracts for her beloved building. And then, *poof*! All their mutual goodwill would disappear.

Crack! Kenny made his shot. Cam grabbed Jordan's hand and held on tight while she sucked in a long, slow breath.

"No!" Luis shouted and sank to his knees, his palm over his chest.

Jordan swerved his attention to the table just in time to see the eight ball sink into the left side pocket.

Cam threw her arms in the air and, in her best announcer voice, shouted, "And *that's* the game!"

She broke into laughter, a sound that rippled down Jordan's spine. When she turned to face him, her face flushed with victory, he forgot about all the negatives he'd been listing in his head only moments ago. She managed to sidle between his legs and collapse into him in a full- frontal hug.

"We won! Woo-hoo!" she exclaimed.

His hand slid into her hair, bringing her lips closer to his. She tilted her head, and the only natural reaction was to kiss her. So he did.

He remembered the taste of her, the feel of her in his arms, and casting sanity to the wind, he indulged his senses in happier times. She melted into him, sitting on his thigh, the way she always would, molding herself into the perfect fit, his perfect match. Because despite their bitter past, despite the ugliness of the last few years without her, she was still his Cam.

"Jeez, you two," Luis admonished, "get a room."

He ignored the jibe and the hoots that erupted around them and held fast to this quicksilver woman. If he broke away, he'd lose her. Right now, right here, he could stop time.

"Ah, so that's how it is," another voice remarked from somewhere outside the realm they'd created.

Time returned, along with reality. And Marcus.

Jordan broke the kiss and stared into Cam's starry eyes with regret. She blinked several times and clumsily got to her feet.

"Sorry," she murmured, her gaze pinned to her sneakers. "Oh, God, I'm sorry. I guess I got carried away. I should go."

She stumbled away from him, headed for the exit.

"No, Cam, wait!" He reached out a hand to stop her, but she kept going. Marcus grabbed her arm as she flew past him, and Jordan saw red. "Keep your hands off her!"

Marcus let go, raising his hands in the air. "It's cool, man. Take it easy. Just answer one question for me. Did we lose the building because of your boss or because of her?"

Cam stopped short, her hand on the doorjamb between the front and the back rooms of the bar. Now, she found the courage to look Jordan in the eye.

He stared directly back at her as he admitted, "Both."

On that one syllable, she bolted.

Chapter 10

"**B**oth! What the hell does that mean?"

Cam paced the floor of her apartment from the windows to the living room to the foyer and back again while an amused Bertie sprawled on her sofa and watched. For two days, she'd stewed over what had happened at Brady's Place. After Jordan made that stupid pronouncement on Friday night, she'd fled the bar, had Danny drive her straight home, and collapsed into bed where she stared at the ceiling until the sun peeked through her blinds on Saturday. The rest of the weekend passed in a blur. She hadn't ventured out of the apartment at all, had in fact, stayed in her ridiculous pajamas, unable to sleep or sit down or erase that two-sentence conversation from her head.

Now, on Sunday evening, when she'd pretty much given up on him, Bertie had showed up at last to talk her down before she wound up round the bend. In her opinion, he'd arrived too late. Her sanity had caught the last bus out of town at least twelve hours ago.

"I mean," she continued, raking fingers through her dirty and disheveled hair at the same frenetic pace as her steps, "really. I don't get it. This guy says, 'Did we lose the building because of your boss or because of her?' and he says, 'Both.' Both what? And what did the other guy mean about losing the building? Do you think he was talking about the building I'm buying? The Loughlin? But what would Jordan want it for? What does his boss have to do with it? And for that matter, what do *I* have to with *any* of this?" She shook her hands around her head. "I didn't come to him with the site; he came to me. If he didn't want me to have it, why bother putting me through all this?"

"Maybe you should ask him," Bertie suggested with a smirk.

Drowning in self-pity, she barely heard him. "I've been agonizing over this deal since I first found out he was the agent. Do you have any idea what it's like to see him, to hold myself back from touching him, and pretend it doesn't hurt? To see him in that chair and want to help, but know any softness I show him will be met with derision? I don't understand why he reached out to me at all. I don't believe for one second he did it for the good of the foundation. He's playing games with me, and I don't know why. Why would he be so cruel? What did I do to make him hate me so much?"

Bertie sat up higher on the couch, all sense of humor gone. "He doesn't hate you. My guess is he's as confused as you are. You two have a history you've never overcome. That's why I told you to have lunch with him. To talk. Clear the air. Start over."

"Yeah, well." She uttered a bitter laugh. "You heard how well that went!"

"So, try again. Somewhere else."

"And risk having him kiss me again?" A snort flew from her nose. "No, thank you!" She stopped, midway in her traverse, her arms loose at her sides. "Did I tell you he kissed me?"

"Yes. Three times. How was it?"

Her guard dropped, and she relived that one moment, touching her mouth, as if she could still feel him there. "It was wonderful. I'd forgotten—" *Wait a minute.* Realizing what he was up to, she glared at Bertie. His cheeks twitched, and she pointed a finger at him. "Are you laughing at me?"

He rounded his eyes, and shook his head in rapid fashion. "I wouldn't dare." At her impatient huff, he patted the cushion beside him. "Sit. You're wearing ruts in the floor with this whirling dervish routine. I'm surprised your shoes haven't caught fire."

For the first time since Friday night, a glimmer of a smile tickled her lips. She picked up her feet to show him the scuffed Converse sneakers. "They're rubber."

"Good. Safety first. Now, sit." He patted the cushion again.

On another huff, she plopped into the seat. "This is all your fault, you know. If you had answered my texts Friday night, I wouldn't have pestered Val and then wound up at her place before—" A sudden fear gripped her. "Crap. That's another problem I totally forgot about. Val's probably gonna quit on Tuesday, and that's your fault, too."

"Of course it is." His tone was flat, unaffected. "Everything's my fault: dinosaur extinction, the Black Plague, climate change, all the miseries of mankind are my fault. Care to tell me why I've compelled Val to quit now?"

"Because when I couldn't reach *you*, I called her."

"Oh, well, sure. That makes sense."

"It does." She tucked her legs underneath her butt and sat sideways on the sofa to face him. "Do you know what I realized the other night?"

"What?"

"That you're my only friend." A tear itched behind her eye, but she sniffed it back. "Isn't that pathetic?"

"Tragic."

Too antsy to stay in one position for long, she straightened her legs, threw herself against the cushioned back of the sofa, and folded her arms over her chest. "You're not funny. I really needed you, and you weren't there for me."

"This may shock you, but I do have a job, Cam. I'm a football coach for the New York Vanguard. You might've heard of them."

She smirked at his attempt at sarcasm. "Ha ha."

"No, really. I've got dozens of grown men who are usually needier than you." He settled an arm around her shoulders. "Not right now, but usually. The kickoff game is a week away, and I couldn't just drop everything because you and your mother had another row. So you called Val. Sounds like you did a smart thing. That lady's been with you long enough. She's seen your ugly side, I'm sure."

She squirmed out of his grasp. "I'm serious. I blew it with her, pushed too much. I practically bulldozed my way into her house."

"Did she say that?"

"No, but I could tell she was uncomfortable with my being there. I'm her boss. In fact, she kept calling me boss the whole time, even when I told her not to. It was all, 'Anything you say, boss; okay, boss; you're the boss.' I felt awful when she fell asleep. I gave her Monday off to recuperate and even offered her a spa treatment from Zahra as an apology. God knows if she'll accept." Clasping her hands in her lap, she dipped her head. "I'm no good with people. Maybe I should get a dog. Or a lizard. Definitely a lizard, something cold-blooded, since, apparently, I'm cold-blooded, too."

"You're one of the warmest people I know. You've just got a lot of barriers. Sounds to me like you tried knocking down a few of them on Friday night. That's a good thing. I'm sure Val thought so, too."

"Yeah, well, I'm not so sure. I just didn't know what else to do. Like I said, when I couldn't reach you..." She glared at him, trying to burn him with the power of her eyes. "I called her. She was planning a nice, quiet night at home with some kind of salmon dish and a bath, and I totally crashed it."

He quirked a brow. "You crashed her bath?"

"No!" She sighed. "Keep up, Bertie. I intruded on her plans for a relaxing evening at home."

"Did you bring work with you for her to do?"

She clucked her tongue. "No, just a pizza. We'd both put in a sixteen-hour day on Friday. I'm not a monster."

"Then, what's the problem?"

"She fell asleep on the couch, and I felt awful that I'd intruded on her, so I left. That's when I went to Brady's Place."

"Where you ran into Jordan, shot a game of pool, kissed him—"

On a gasp, she slapped the space between them. "I did not kiss him!"

"Where *he* kissed you," he amended, "while you struggled to retain your honor."

"Well, not exactly, but..." She dipped her head. "Okay."

"Then some big guy walked in and made a comment about a building and you ran out. And that's where we're at now."

"Yes." She waited, but he said nothing more. "Well?"

"Well what?"

"What do you think it means?"

"I don't know. Ask Jordan." He pulled her against him again, and this time, she didn't fight. "Just do me a favor? Shower first. Brush your hair—and your teeth. And put on clean pajamas."

She yawned as exhaustion finally claimed her. Snuggled into Bertie's broad chest, his heartbeat thumping against her ear, she whispered, "Okay," and promptly fell asleep.

EARLY TUESDAY MORNING, Jordan greeted Marcus outside the empty space that had once housed the Stalk Food Store and Farmers' Market. "Thanks for coming."

"How could I not? You sounded pretty excited on the phone."

After Cam had run off the other night, he sensed Marcus was about to do the same. So had everyone else inside Brady's Place, which sent them all into raucous laughter.

"What happened, Wheels?" Luis admonished. "Was Cam not impressed with your technique? Maybe we should play another game. Your charm seems to be wearing off."

"Worst response to kissing a woman I've ever seen," Kenny added. "You couldn't even get her to stay out of pity."

That remark got Marcus's back up. The sports physical therapist did not take kindly to anyone ridiculing his clients. Fists at his sides, he stalked forward, intent on pounding some respect into the man. "You listen to me, you little weasel—"

"Marcus!" Jordan cut off the brewing fight. "Forget him. He's harmless." He jerked his head toward the front area. "Come on. Let's go up front where we can talk."

Marcus shifted his weight to one hip and folded his arms over his chest. "Forget about it. Call me tomorrow or something."

Jordan pushed forward toward the doorway, hoping he could convince Marcus to stay long enough to hear him out. "No, I can't forget about it. I need to explain. Please."

To Jordan's relief, on a disgruntled huff of air, Marcus followed him to the front of the bar. Jordan gestured to the same booth he'd shared with Cam. Once they were seated, he ordered a beer for Marcus, another ginger ale for himself.

Only after the drinks were on the table and he was assured there'd be no additional interruptions did he open the conversation again. "What you walked in on back there, it's not what it seemed."

Marcus took a swig of his beer, but his expression remained impassive. "Uh-huh. Sure. 'Cuz it looked to me like you were sucking face with the enemy."

"She's not the enemy." He rolled his eyes, sipped his ginger ale, and gathered his thoughts. "Look, like it or not, Cam and I have a history. We didn't have a great ending, but when we were good together, we were really good together. Tonight, she'd been drinking, and we shot a game of pool, and the music and the game and the atmosphere stirred up some fond memories. That's all it was."

Marcus narrowed his eyes and tilted his bottle toward Jordan. "So you two were lip-locked when I walked in out of some kind of weird moment of nostalgia?"

"Of course."

Either that, or Kenny was right and she'd kissed him out of pity. Because she had definitely responded with enthusiasm when he'd kissed her. Question was, did she respond honestly or had she put on a show to make him feel better about himself?

He had to hope for the former. But he couldn't completely discount the latter. Maybe she had ignored him all these years because she couldn't bear having to see him confined to a chair? Not such an odd theory. He'd hated it at first, too. Had avoided mirrors for close to a year, in fact. Well, to hell with that. Cam could keep her pity for someone who needed it. Not him.

"Okay," Marcus replied. "Let's say I buy that explanation."

"What's to buy? It's the truth."

"Theresa thinks you still love her."

God, had he let so much of his guard down at Marcus's place last week? He shook his head but couldn't verbalize a more emphatic denial.

Marcus ignored him. "So that makes me wonder where you and I stand. It's why I asked you if we lost the building because of your boss or because of her. I mean, if someone else representing the Delgado Foundation had been in charge of the acquisition, would you have let it go so easily?"

"Absolutely."

"No hesitation," Marcus remarked. "How can you be so sure?"

Because it's the truth, his saner self had replied.

Oh, sure. Susan might have been the instigator of this whole conundrum, but if he really didn't want Cam to have the site, he could've said no. Her threats to fire him were empty. He didn't need the job. Not financially. He had plenty of money in the bank, most of it earmarked for this project with Marcus. If Susan did fire him, he could easily transition from corporate real estate to handling the books for the therapy business when it was up and running. He wouldn't be as happy, stuck in an office all day without the ability to get outside every once in a while, but he could do it. Or he could find another realtor to join, despite Susan's threat to blackball him. In fact, he could think of several realty companies who'd see Susan's animosity as a selling point.

As for Cam, the minute he saw her walking around the interior of the Loughlin site, he'd known it was meant for her. It might have been years since they'd been together, but he still knew her moods, her priorities, and her goals. Hope had lit up her eyes and for that moment, he saw the place the way he sensed she did: full of kids and laughter and joy.

Just as he saw this old supermarket as the perfect spot for him and Marcus: full of people working hard to create a new normal, thanks to a split-second event that had shattered their lives. As he'd noticed on the listing website, the space was in a great location, had plenty of space—all on one floor, which was a huge plus for him and others like him—a large parking area, and came well within budget.

He looked up at Marcus now, framing his forehead with the back of his hand to block out the brutal sun his shades failed to repel. "What do you think?"

"It's definitely better suited to our needs than the other place," Marcus agreed.

"And there'd probably be room for a pool," Jordan added.

Hydrotherapy was crucial for some injuries. A pool would be a huge bonus they wouldn't have dared consider at the other site. Still, it was best he didn't make promises he might not be able to keep.

"I'll know more about what we can and can't do once I get my hands on the specs."

Marcus glanced at him. "What's holding that up?"

"Susan," he admitted with a frown. She's not the selling agent for this property. Which makes this transaction..." He swallowed hard. "...delicate."

"Delicate or impossible?"

"Nothing's impossible. It's just a question of drawing her in the right way. But I wanted to make sure we were ready to pursue the site before I get her involved."

Because despite Michaela and Rachel trying to convince him otherwise, he would not go behind her back to chase this space. He'd only get serious about it if he got Marcus's okay and Susan's blessing. If either refused to give him what he needed, he'd look elsewhere. In business and in his personal life, Jordan wanted loyalty. He'd give no less in return.

"So, what do you think?" he pressed. "Are we interested in seeing more?"

"Yeah, I think so. What happens next?"

Jordan forced a grim smile. "I have to convince Susan to help us."

Chapter 11

When Cam strode into work on Tuesday morning, she half-expected Val's area to have been stripped bare. But no. Not only was Val's stuff still there, a sunny, smiling Val sat behind her desk.

"Good morning! Thanks for the spa package yesterday. It was a really nice surprise. That massage was ah-maz-ing!"

So convinced was she that she'd screwed up her relationship with Val, a dumbstruck Cam could barely speak when she found her assumption dead wrong. "Oh, good. I'm... er... glad you enjoyed it. What... what are you doing here?"

"It's Tuesday. Your note said come back on Tuesday." Her face drained of color. "Oh, God! Am I *fired*?" She whispered the last word with enough dread to chill the air.

Relief flooded through Cam, and she laughed. "No. Not at all. In fact, grab some coffee and come into my office."

Val remained dubious. "If it's about the notepads in my drawer, I can explain."

"Val, relax." She strode toward her office door. "You're not fired. I promise. This is good news. Join me when you're ready. We've got a lot of stuff to cover."

Pushing inside, she let the door swing wide and stay open. Cam settled at her desk and booted up her computer, then accessed Val's HR file. She'd already reviewed the numbers and the details, but she wanted to keep them fresh in her mind.

A pale Val crept into the office, eyes downcast at the utilitarian gray carpet, and Cam hid a smile. She hovered there, halfway between the desk and the door, as if she wanted an equal distance between her future and her past. Amusement lifted Cam's mood, but she feigned a sternness just to toy with Val for a second or two. It would make the outcome that much more delicious for both of them. At least, she hoped so.

"Have a seat, Val."

"Should I shut the door?"

"No, leave it open for now. This won't take long."

Val stumbled into the chair across from Cam's desk and clasped her fingers, settling her hands in her skirted lap. Even so, Cam saw how they trembled.

"First," Cam said, "I want to apologize for barging in on you on Friday night."

Val's head shot up, and her eyes went wide. "You didn't. Honest. When you called, I thought it would be fun, you know? I mean, when we're on these trips like Atlanta, we spend so much time working, we both usually just order room service alone in the hotel at night and crash 'til the next day when we do it all again. Then on the plane home, you always wind up working on... whatever you need to work on, and this time around, I was putting together the prizes for the next fundraiser, so we didn't talk at all. Friday night, when I said let's have a pajama party, I was kidding at first. I mean, I thought you were kidding about coming over. Then, when I realized you were serious and why, I thought, 'Why not?' It could be a blast. I really wanted us to have a chance to let our guards down and just be friends. I'm sorry I fell asleep, but it wasn't because I didn't want you there."

She'd forgotten how Val could ramble. "Let me finish, please."

Val ducked her head again. "Sorry."

"There's no reason to apologize. I'm the one who's sorry. I intruded on your plans for a quiet evening. But that's not why you're here."

"It's not?"

"No, it's not. Val, you've been doing great work here, and I've come to rely on you more than you probably realize—more than I sometimes realize. The acquisition of the Loughlin building is primarily due to your dedication to that project. You're a valuable asset to the foundation and to me. Therefore, I'm prepared to promote you. You'll no longer be my executive assistant. As of this morning, you are the assistant director. You'll be getting an increase in your salary commensurate with your new title." She scribbled the number on a yellow sticky note and slid it forward.

Val's eyes went wide as she looked at the salary written on the paper and then up at Cam. "Is this for real?"

Cam nodded. "I'll be passing more of the day to day work to you from now on, so I hope you're ready to take on more responsibility. Casey will take your place as my executive assistant, and you and I will be hiring you an assistant, also. I'll need you to spend a week or two training Casey to get him up and running, but we'll use that time to familiarize you with some of what you'll be taking on, as well as getting your office set up."

Now, her head came up level and stayed there. Pride and excitement gave her the confidence to sit up straight and look Cam in the eye. "I'm getting an office?"

"Yes. Right next to this one. Does that mean you'd like to accept the offer?"

"Are you kidding? Yes! I mean, this is amazing. Thank you! I can't—" She giggled. "I thought for sure I was getting fired today. I even brought in a box to take my stuff home in."

"Well, now you can use that box to move your stuff into your new office. But before you do that..." She sobered and handed Val the typed-up offer she'd printed earlier this morning. "I'm going to be relying on you for a lot. You'll be well compensated, but there'll be nights you won't get out of here until eight or nine o'clock. Or you'll have to make last minute changes to a print order or the website over the weekend. Be sure to read this over carefully. Take it to an attorney. Don't use the foundation's legal reps. Get an outside opinion from someone with your best interests in mind. We'll make it all official once you've had some time to have this reviewed and bring it back to me signed. Until then, we'll continue on as we have for a while. Okay? Sound good?"

"Are you kidding? It sounds great! Ohmigod, I'm stunned. I really don't know what to say except thank you."

Cam smiled. "Thank you is enough. Now, tuck that agreement into your purse for later, and let's get back to work. I want you to check in on Atlanta, see how the school supply event went. From eleven to about two, I'll be out of the box. You can use those few hours to grab lunch for yourself and start shopping for a lawyer to review that paperwork. Have the fee billed here. This afternoon, we'll go over the details for the Loughlin acquisition. I want you in on all the meetings and conference calls from now on."

Val's jaw dropped. "You sure?"

"I'm sure. This is your baby. You should be there for delivery. Besides, I can't think of anything better than working side by side with a good friend."

A beaming grin lit up Val's face. "Wow. Ditto. Thanks, Cam. This means a lot to me."

"Me, too."

ONCE BACK IN THE OFFICE, Jordan wasted no time in asking Susan to make time for him on her calendar. He then waited until Thursday to actually meet with her. While he would've preferred to get it over with faster, like ripping off a Band-Aid, he used the days in between to argue with himself over what he'd say that wouldn't result in her ousting him from her office and the company.

When he finally entered her inner sanctum that afternoon, she got right to the point.

"What can I do for you, Jordan? Not a problem with the Delgado deal, I hope." She stood, leaning a hip against the edge of her desk, her navy blazer draped over her shoulders and her fists planted on her slim hips, the ultimate power pose.

Hell, if there were a problem with the Delgado deal, with her connections, she'd know before he did. He wouldn't have a clue 'til she sliced his head from his shoulders.

Still, he played along. "All systems go there. No, this is more of a... personal matter."

She nodded. "Right. The supermarket site on 57th."

He goggled at her. "How'd you know?"

Her lips twisted into a smirk. "Do you honestly think anything goes on in this office I'm not privy to?"

Apparently not. "So, what do you think?"

The smirk became a crocodile smile: predatory and dangerous. "What do *you* think?"

Tread carefully.

He chose his words with purpose, exactly as he'd rehearsed them for the last two days. "I'd like to pursue the possibility of acquiring it. I won't know if I'm definitely interested until I contact the selling agent and discuss some of the site's details. I'll need specs, particularly of the interior layout. It's a bigger space, which allows for more possibilities for what we want to do, but possibilities becoming realities will depend on a lot of X factors. Right now, Marcus and I've only checked out the exterior. Who can say if it's going to be the right property for us until we've done our homework?"

She folded her arms over her chest, her posture deceptively languid. "You haven't contacted the agent yet?"

"No."

"But you know who the agent is?"

"Yes."

"And you still have the gall to come to me."

He held up a hand to stem the tide of vipers or locusts she planned to send his way. "I won't do anything unless you're okay with my doing business with that particular firm."

He didn't have to say the name; they both understood the identity of the agent and why there was an issue. Why rub salt into Susan's open wound?

"But before you say no or threaten to toss me off the GW Bridge for daring to even ask, I thought you might want to consider representing my and my partner's interests in the transaction."

The first crack in her veneer appeared. Her eyes widened just a bit, then narrowed again. "Why? You're quite capable of representing yourself."

"That's true. But then, you wouldn't get the lion's share of the commission or the opportunity to show your ex-partner that you're still at the top of your game."

Her posture relaxed, and she whipped the blazer off her shoulders, tossing it onto the seat of her chair. "You know, should you decide to pursue this, I'm going to low ball the crap out of her. I will cut her into a thousand pieces and bury her in paperwork. It could be months before this deal is done."

He shrugged with nonchalance. "I figured as much."

With her hands now clutching the edges of her desk, she leaned forward at the waist. "Your partner's okay with you wasting valuable time to entertain me?"

"He's allowing me to run this deal as I see fit."

"And you see fit to let me play in your sandbox so I can get some misguided revenge." He nodded. "Why?"

"Because we all have to face our demons at one point. You made me face mine by pushing me to handle the Delgado deal. I thought I wasn't ready. I kept telling myself I'd face Cam when I was as successful as she is. Without your prodding, I'm not sure I would've ever been ready. Because the truth is, I might never be as successful as she is—at least, not in the business world. In my personal life, I've conquered mountains most people don't dare climb. That makes me successful in my own right."

He pointed at her. "You gave me back my self-confidence to see myself as Cam's equal—not because of the money in my bank account, but because after all life threw at me, I'm still standing." He glanced down at himself in the chair. "Figuratively speaking, of course. Now I'm going to give you the opportunity to face your demon. If you want it."

"Oh, I want it. But you already knew I would, didn't you?"

"If I say yes, will that get you onboard faster?"

Her laughter scraped his spine. The last thing he'd ever want is to make this woman an enemy. She was a much better ally anyway.

"I'm onboard, regardless. Now I know how you got Cam Delgado on your side. You take no prisoners. I'm impressed."

Good thing Cam wasn't around to hear that praise. He doubted she'd agree. Funny. He hadn't considered how much facing her and putting this deal together had meant to his well-being until he'd verbalized it for his boss. But he meant every word he said.

Cam hadn't been his demon after all. The dragon he'd been forced to slay was his own stubborn pride.

Chapter 12

Two weeks later, Cam looked around from the head of the table in the foundation's larger conference room. Val sat to her immediate right in her first official task as assistant director, flanked by the foundation's team of lawyers and financial officers. They all, even Val, wore expressions of cool confidence. All except Cam.

Despite her simple emerald silk tee and white linen slacks, she couldn't get comfortable and squirmed in her seat, seeking a position that would ease the tension building up inside her. A wave of heat bathed her skin, leaving a light sheen of sweat to bead her pounding forehead. Her insides tumbled in freefall. Her symptoms didn't come from any lack of air conditioning or a fever. Nor was she nervous about the transaction. No, her discomfort came from the presence of one man.

Jordan sat with his legal representatives to her left. She hadn't seen him since that night at Brady's Place, the night he'd kissed her. A tingle lingered on her lips whenever she recalled that moment.

God help her, she still loved him. Would always love him. She wouldn't tell him, couldn't humiliate herself to bear his laughter when he told her he'd lost interest in her years ago.

Closing off her misery behind her walls of business senses, she faced him with a steady gaze. He stared back, unblinking, and yet, unsure. Maybe that kiss hadn't affected him as much as it did her, or maybe he experienced some small whisper of remorse at how their relationship had imploded. God knew, she felt it.

With all the details hammered out at last, she picked up the gold fountain pen her father always used to sign his contracts and put the nib to the first line requiring her authorization. She'd just started the arc in C when the interoffice unit buzzed.

"Cam?" Casey's uncertain voice broke into the silence of the boardroom. "Sorry to interrupt. I got an emergency call from the stadium. Something's happened to Bertie. He's been taken to Regional Hospital."

The pen fell from her fingers with a clatter as she shot to her feet. Panic coursed through her veins, tightened her chest, and stole her breath, but she didn't stop her forward momentum. From behind her fleeing figure, she heard Val announce into the speaker with crisp efficiency, "Casey, have someone bring a car out front."

"Already done," Casey replied. "Larry's waiting downstairs."

A high-pitched buzz blaring in Cam's head drowned out anything else said in the conference room. She pushed out the door and raced past the elevator to the stairs. Later, when asked, she wouldn't recall how she made it down the dozen flights, out to the street, or anything she said to her driver before he opened the door again in front of the hospital's entrance. Minor details became a blur. All that mattered was reaching Bertie.

Once inside the emergency room, she barely took in the groupings of people seated around the waiting area. She raced straight to the reception desk where a dark-haired nurse sat at a desk behind a wall of Plexiglas. When the nurse didn't look up right away at her approach, Cam used her fingernail to tap on the barrier.

With an annoyed expression on her face, the nurse slid the window to one side. "Can I help you?"

"Bertie—Albert Wallace," she told the woman through gasps for breath. "He came in by ambulance a while ago."

"Are you family?"

"I'm his daughter," she replied.

The nurse turned to her computer and entered in some information, then looked up at Cam again. "Your name?"

"Cameron. Cameron Delgado."

She pointed to the waiting room with its clusters of strangers. "Have a seat. Dr. Ferrone will be out in a few minutes."

Cam gripped the counter in front of her. "How is he? Can I see him?"

"Have a seat, please." *Scriiiiitch*! She slid the window closed again.

With no other choice, Cam walked to a row of chairs and perched on the edge of the closest seat to the double-doors that read Authorized Personnel

Only. Her legs shook, her heartbeat thundered in her ears, and a hitch in her throat made her breathing ragged. What had happened to Bertie? An injury on the field? An injury like Jordan's? Couldn't be. Bertie was a coach. The much-younger players took the hits and did the work these days. He just yelled a lot and blew a whistle. And sometimes got in the way because he was stubborn and thought he knew best.

Oh, God. What if he was really hurt? She straightened her spine. Well, then, she'd take care of him. Just like she would've done with Jordan if he'd wanted. Because that was what you did for the people you loved.

She glanced at the clock above the nurse's head behind that stupid window. 4:54 pm.

How long would she have to wait before she could see him? Where was he? Was he in surgery? Were they running tests? Would he be staying overnight? Longer?

The doors remained closed. No answers came.

Around her, other people looked at their phones while they waited on these uncomfortable hard chairs. She couldn't be bothered to pull her phone out of her purse. Why would she? She didn't want to see the text messages from coworkers asking for details she didn't have yet. Another glance at the clock.

4:54 pm.

Aaaargh! How could that be? She'd been sitting here forever already! Was the clock broken? Maybe that was why everyone stared at their phones. To keep track of the time. She twisted her fingers round and round, tried to watch the television mounted in the corner of the room, turned to local news. Nothing penetrated her brain. She dared another glance at the clock.

4:55 pm.

Oh, come on! This was ridiculous.

At last, the doors hissed open, and a man in scrubs strode out, stopping at the nurse's window. She skooched until more of her bottom was off the chair's edge than on. The two spoke, the side wall barring Cam from seeing the doctor's expression or reading his lips. Not that she could read lips. The man left the nurse's area. Cam's breath caught. He walked back through the double doors. Cam deflated.

4:59 pm.

This was excruciating!

The nurse slid her window open again. Cam shot up. "Blankenship?" A man and a woman with a toddler on her hip rose from their chairs and headed forward. "You can go on back to Exam Room Three."

With a sharp buzz, the doors opened, and the family disappeared into the inner sanctum.

5:06 pm.

The doors swished open again, and this time a woman in scrubs came out, calling "Wallace?"

For a minute, Cam didn't move, but then her brain kicked in and she realized the woman was referring to Bertie. She shot up, her arm straight in the air. "Here!"

She sped forward, and the woman escorted her through the double doors, but stopped once they were inside a vast room separated by curtained areas with numbered signs hanging from the ceiling.

The noise, the smells, the frenetic activity swirled around her, but she kept her focus on the woman speaking.

"Ms. Delgado, I'm sorry to have to tell you this. Mr. Wallace suffered a massive heart attack on the field at Vanguard Stadium. He died before medical personnel could arrive and resuscitate him."

She listened to this stranger's empty condolences, numb with grief. *I'm very sorry. It was sudden and quick. I can assure you, he felt little to no pain.*

Really? How could Dr. Whoever know that? Did Bertie die with a big grin on his face? Were his last words, "Hey, you know what? This isn't half bad."? She clamped her jaws around the retort and reined in her temper with effort. Blasting this poor doctor or nurse or clerk or whoever she was for having to deliver the news to her would help no one.

"Can I see him?" she asked instead.

With a solemn nod, the woman led her past the emergency area and into a private room where the shell of Albert "Bertie" Wallace lay, growing colder and more ashen as time elapsed.

He was gone.

She didn't have to touch him to know that the dynamo in perpetual motion, the bear of a man who had bolstered her through some of her darkest days, no longer existed in this realm. She bent to place her head against his chest. The heartbeat that used to thrum like a lullaby made no sound. She lifted his hand to kiss it and stifled a shiver at the waxy cold feel of his flesh against her lips.

An anguished cry ripped from her soul. "Oh, Bertie! What will I do without you?"

The woman cleared her throat and dragged a heavy cushioned chair closer to the bedside. "I'll give you some time."

She walked away, closing the door behind her as she left.

God knew how long Cameron sat alone inside this barren room, weeping softly and recalling all the moments she'd shared with Bertie, good and bad. Had she told him she loved him the last time they'd spoken? She couldn't remember.

"I love you," she said now. "I love you, I love you, I love you." She repeated the same three words until her throat ached and a white-haired nurse arrived to escort her from the room.

"We'll take care of him now," she murmured, patting Cam's hand.

Cameron struggled to get up out of the chair, her gaze never leaving her fallen hero.

"Go on," the nurse prompted. "I promise. He's in good hands. He's with the angels now."

A smile quirked Cam's tight lips. Bertie, the atheist, would probably *love* to hear this news.

"There now, see. I bet you hadn't thought of that. Gives you some peace, don't it?"

More like a fit of the giggles, but she left the room nonetheless, and nearly tripped over Jordan hovering in the hallway.

"Cam?"

She didn't have to say a word. Good thing, since she couldn't say it aloud yet. Saying it aloud would confirm the finality in her heart, and she wasn't ready.

"Aw, Cam, I'm sorry. I'm so sorry."

Blinded by tears, she stumbled toward the nearby waiting area and collapsed into the same hard plastic chair she'd sat in a lifetime ago—Bertie's lifetime ago. Jordan rolled up beside her, took her icy hand in his warmer one, and squeezed gently. The floodgates on Cam's emotions broke open, and she wept.

"I was too late. I never even got to say goodbye. He was gone before I got here—before *he* got here. I didn't have a chance to tell him how much I loved him, how much he meant to me. He died not knowing he was my hero."

"He knew, sweetheart. He always knew. Just like you've always known how much he loved you. You two had a special bond. That didn't change when he died."

She looked up at him, noted the tenderness in his expression—not pity; he knew she couldn't abide pity. Empathy and his own devastation at the news reflected in his steady gaze. Her lips parted of their own accord, and she leaned toward him, hungry for the connection they once shared. Hungry for life. He understood her need and met her halfway, his breath growing warmer near her cheek.

Into this soft and touching moment, her stomach made itself known with a growl that would shame a grizzly.

He jerked back. "When's the last time you ate?"

Cheeks flaming, she shook her head. "I don't remember. Sometime yesterday."

He gave her hand another squeeze. "Well, you're going to need lots of protein to keep up your strength for all that's coming. I assume Larry's waiting downstairs?" At her nod, he whipped out his phone. "Are all the extensions for the driving service still the same?" Another nod, and he scrolled with a finger.

If she'd had full control of her senses, she would've asked why he continued to have the contact information for the foundation's car service in his phone after all these years, but right now, the only thought in her mind was gratitude that someone else took care of the detritus of banal living while she stayed numb, cocooned in grief.

"Larry, it's Jordan Fawcett." Pause. "Same here." Another pause. "I'm afraid the news isn't good, but it's not my place to say. Ms. Delgado and I are on our way down. Take her home, bring her around the back. I'm not sure if the press has the news in their nostrils yet, but just in case, let's not push her into a melee. I'll follow you to her place and get her comfortable. If luck's on our side, she can be safe upstairs before the news gets out. While I'm taking care of her, would you mind driving over to the Grille Room and picking up a takeout order for us? I'll place the order now, so you'll have some time before it'll be ready." Pause. "Terrific. Thanks."

The orders punctuated the dense fog in Cam's head, but she couldn't form a coherent thought on her own.

While she sat lost in her mourning tomb, he placed a second call to the Grille Room. He never asked for her opinion before he ordered two porterhouse steaks, a side of asparagus spears, two baked potatoes topped with sour cream and chives, and for dessert, a slice of chocolate ganache cake. He did, however, throw a questioning glance her way before disconnecting, and she responded with an unenthusiastic thumbs-up. She wouldn't change a thing he'd ordered. It was disconcerting to realize he knew all her food weaknesses—all her weaknesses, period.

While she would've liked to argue with him, the truth was, her stomach could use a refill and the next few days were going to be hell. So, why not let him take care of her for a little while? What harm could it do?

The devastating news hit her anew. Bertie was gone. And, despite Jordan's current position beside her, eventually, he'd return to... wherever and whomever he had in his orbit. But *her* life had irrevocably changed. For the first time since that devastating night nearly thirty years ago when her dad died, she was alone again.

"Let's get you home, Cam."

SHE PASSED ON THE CHOCOLATE cake, which had always been her favorite dessert.

"Try a bite," he cajoled, waving a small portion of the treat speared on his fork.

With a shake of her head, she refused his offer, then gestured at the dirty takeout dishes from their meal scattered across the tabletop. "Thanks for the dinner, but I think I need to be by myself for a while."

It didn't take a brain surgeon to see she was fragile right now. At the same time, though, Jordan probably wasn't high on the list of people she'd turn to for comfort and solace. Unfortunately, the man she most needed was the one who'd died. And Jordan knew without being told, he was a poor substitute for Bertie.

"Will you be all right?" he asked. "Is there somebody I can call to stay with you?"

She pushed away from the bistro table and got to her unsteady feet. A major yawn widened her mouth. "I just want a hot bath and some sleep."

He gave her a hard stare, and she clucked her tongue. "What? Don't look at me like that. I'll be okay. Honest. I'm broken but not beaten. I'll survive."

"Glad to hear it." He stared out the window at the Manhattan skyline, where darkness began to drop and lights clicked on in odd patterns in the other buildings. Clearing his facial expression of any obvious concern took some time—particularly since that last phrase was pure Bertie, and he wondered if she realized she used it.

His gaze traveled back to her in time to see her hands twisting in front of her stomach. "Can I ask a favor though?"

"Sure."

"Will you ride with me to the memorial service? I know it might not be comfortable for you, that there might be some bad blood between you and some of your former teammates, but..." Her voice cracked, and she looked at him through red-rimmed, wet eyes. "I can't do this alone."

He nodded. "If you want me there, I'll be there. No matter what anyone else says." Not that his former teammates had any grudge against him anyway. They'd understood his reason for leaving. Everyone had—everyone but Cam.

"No one will *say* anything. I'll make sure of it. Well, except my mom." She picked up a remote control from the glass-topped end table and pointed it at the window. On a low hum, horizontal shades slid downward, dimming the light in the living room and covering the view. "Her, I have no control over. She's a damn tornado in an outhouse."

Another Bertie phrase. He had no idea if she was channeling the dead man or if Bertie's spirit had refused to leave its earthly bonds and had taken up residence in Cam. To hell with masking his concern. She needed someone here with her tonight.

"How about I spend the night?" he said, keeping his tone light.

Her eyes bugged out and a grimace twisted her lips. She toed off her shoes before replying on a huff of air, "Get real."

"On the couch," he added. "You won't even know I'm here."

He'd be up all night, since there was no way he could sleep anywhere but his own custom bed these days, but she didn't need to know that. What she needed was to have a sounding board nearby, someone to watch over her, to be ready to catch her when she crumbled tonight. Because she *would* crumble.

She bent to pick up her shoes, saying nothing, and he pressed his advantage. "Why don't you go change and I'll make coffee?"

Taking a few steps toward the bedroom, she tossed over her shoulder, "Go home, Jordan. I'm fine. I don't need a babysitter."

"Definitely not, but I don't think Bertie would want you to be alone tonight, either."

On a quick whirl, she speared him with a gaze blazing arrows of anger. "Who made you an expert on what Bertie would want? When was the last time you talked to him? Five years ago?"

"More like a few weeks ago, actually."

Her posture sagged, and the fire dimmed in her eyes. "Oh, right. You guys talked football, didn't you?"

"*He* talked football. I talked about you."

"Why?" The single syllable came out a harsh whisper, roughened by doubt and grief. Her voice trembled on the edge of tears, but she didn't let them fall. She never did—not if anyone else was around. She'd grow brittle, but she never let a crack appear in her strong veneer.

"Why did I talk about you?"

She dropped her shoes with a thud. Tossing her head to shake out her hair, she fisted her hands at her sides. Jordan knew the signs and braced for impact. *Here it comes. The breakdown.*

He might not have seen one from her in a few years, but he never forgot how they started—or how they usually ended—with the two of them snuggled in bed. Well, *that part* wasn't about to happen. Not tonight. Not ever again. No way he'd let her get that close to him ever again.

He would help her through the next few days, seal the deal on the Loughlin site, and then get the hell away from her before his heart could become engaged. Not for her. He wasn't that philanthropic—or crazy. No, he'd do this for Bertie. For Susan. For Marcus. And for himself.

"Yes. Why?" Eyes narrowed, she stalked closer, a panther spotting weak prey. "Why did you talk about me? And while you're at it, tell me why you came back to New York. Why did you call me about that building? Why couldn't you just leave me alone? Why didn't you go away and *stay* away? Do you have any idea how seeing you like this makes me feel?"

Seeing you like this. Wow. While he'd expected the attack, her method, accusing him of trying to stir some kind of pity out of her because he was in a chair, rankled.

"Then don't look at me. Or pretend I'm someone you never knew before I brought you that property. Forget we have any kind of history. You're very good at forgetting about people."

"What's that supposed to mean?"

At her demand, reason returned. What the hell was he doing? He was supposed to be talking her down, not pushing her closer to the edge.

"Nothing," he muttered and ran a hand through his hair to calm his temper. "Go change. I can't imagine you're comfortable in that starchy linen suit combo. Try to find something soft and loose in that massive walk-in closet of yours. Meanwhile, I'll make coffee, and maybe then, you'll be up for a few bites of chocolate. The next few days are gonna suck. Take your kindnesses where you can for now. Time enough for fighting when we've gotten through all this."

"Don't patronize me," she grumbled, but the bite had already disappeared from her tone.

He clutched his chest in mock outrage. "Me? Never."

A glimmer of a smile eased her features, defusing the tension in the room. "Ass."

"Where you're concerned," he replied, his timbre soft but solid as steel, "always."

She cocked her head, staring at him as if seeing him for the first time. Who knew? Maybe she was.

He studied her back, noted the way she pulled at her fingers, spotted the moisture glistening in her eyes. Vulnerability peeked through her rough-and-tumble veneer, and he sighed. "When I'm sure you'll be all right here on your own, I'll leave. Whether that takes five minutes or five days. No ulterior motives. I'm a shoulder you can cry on or lean on. Don't question it; just accept the offer for what it is. Okay?"

"Okay," she murmured. "Thanks."

After picking up her shoes, she wandered into the back of the apartment toward the bedroom. Once she was out of sight, he glanced up at the ceiling. He wondered if Bertie had received his halo yet. Dealing with Cam over the last thirty years, he'd earned it. Who would take care of her now? Not that she was some helpless waif—far from it. But he knew her challenges as well as he knew his own. Who would remind her how beautiful, how accomplished, how *spectacular* she was, when self-doubt crippled her?

Despite the passage of time, he still knew every inch of this apartment. Rolling around her kitchen evoked memories of nights spent cooking pasta and drinking wine, mornings with omelets and orange juice, of birthday celebrations, holidays, and quiet rainy afternoons filled with laughter and passion. Where had they gone so wrong?

By the time she returned, he had the coffeepot set up, mugs on the counter, and the bistro table cleared of everything but the single piece of cake and two forks.

"Thanks." Her tone was still stifled to whisper soft, as if too much emotion might escape should she loosen the release valve. "You were right. I didn't realize how much I needed this." She gestured to the old, heather gray Vanguard t-shirt and black cotton shorts she'd donned.

He nodded. Maybe they could keep everything civil now. For both their sakes. "Coffee will be up in a few minutes. Take a seat."

While he grabbed two mugs from the stand on the counter, she returned to the bistro table. "Thanks, Jordan. I'm sorry I've been so—"

The elevator dinged, and she whirled in surprise. The doors slid open, and Jordan's hopes for a peaceful evening took a swan dive into a cement floor. Into the eye of the storm strode her mother, reanimating the anxiety in the air into frenzy.

Cam shot to her feet, all trace of calm withered from her posture and expression. The face-off resembled a television sitcom. Six-foot-tall Cameron, barefoot and in her t-shirt and shorts, resembled some ancient Amazon compared to her rail-thin, diminutive mother in a navy suit and leather pumps, a sapphire and diamond necklace with a matching cuff bracelet glinting off the overhead lights.

"How'd you get in here, Mother?"

"Don't blame Scott downstairs. He said he had to announce me, but once I told him about Bertie dying, he understood you needed me right now and agreed to send me right up."

"You told Scott? Why? The foundation planned to release a statement to the press tomorrow morning. Now, I guarantee you the press not only knows, but they're going to be camped out in the lobby within the next fifteen minutes."

Her mother waved her left hand, and the setting sun caught the wedding set on her third finger, nearly blinding Jordan with its brilliance. Good Lord, it was a wonder she didn't set the drapes on fire.

"I can well imagine the press release you're planning. All about Saint Albert Wallace and his holy hands and how no one can ever take his place." She sniffed her disdain, a sound he remembered all too well.

"God, you're petty! You just can't stand to let Bertie have the dignified end he deserved, can you? Somehow, you have to make yourself the star of this tragedy, all because he didn't adore you enough when you were married. What'd you tell Scott anyway? How devastated you are? Did you describe in great detail the pain Bertie's death causes *you*?"

"Don't be ridiculous." She wagged a finger toward Cam's nose, and Cam took a step back to avoid any potential contact. "If you didn't have rules in place that I'm not allowed up here without your permission, I wouldn't need to tell anybody down there anything. But, noooo. You want to keep some modicum of power between us by erecting guardrails, as if I mean you harm. You treat me like I'm an axe murderer, for God's sake."

She might as well be, in Jordan's opinion. Like an axe murderer, Laurel wanted to cut her daughter down every chance she got, blow by careless blow. Cam tightened her lips, no doubt to control the words coming from her mouth. When she spoke again, she managed to keep her tone even and at a reasonable volume.

"I live alone in a place where the elevator opens up into my living room. I don't have a front door I can lock. My security is the guard downstairs. That means I take precautions. *No one* comes up without my being notified first. That's just common sense and standard procedure for anyone who has a place like mine."

"Don't blame me for your poor choices in life. You're thirty-six years old. I haven't been responsible for your marital status, where you live, or how you look for a long time."

Cam's temper would no longer remain tethered. "Get out. Get out of my home, and don't come back. I'm done with you."

Laurel stomped a spiked heel. "How dare you!"

Whoa. Time to break this up. Jordan rolled forward into the fray. "Easy, Cam. You're not thinking clearly right now—"

"Stay out of this, Jordan. This is between me and her." Cam's eyes, blazing with fire, cut to him before returning to the target of her ire. "Bertie always insisted I give you the benefit of the doubt. With him gone, I no longer have to heed that advice. I don't have to respect you because you're my mother, especially when you've gone out of your way to disrespect me and all I've loved my whole life. I'm over it: the drama, the snide comments about my size and looks, and most of all, the insults about Bertie. He was the best thing that ever happened to us after Dad died, but you never appreciated him. The whole time he was alive, I put up with your crap and let you criticize every breath I took because I had his love to fall back on when you made me feel bad about myself. But he's gone now. And any desire to continue fostering this toxic relationship between us died with him."

Cam's voice was whisper-soft, laced with steel. Under normal circumstances, he'd admire the way she kept control of her emotions, particularly because he knew the history she alluded to. Bertie might have died, but the spirit and confidence he'd instilled in Cameron lived on—along with a little too much fight for today.

When Cam's hands curled into fists, the tension in the room ratcheted up a notch. For a scary moment, he wondered if she'd physically pick up her mother to toss her out of the apartment.

Apparently, Laurel shared his fear, because her complexion paled, and she looked his way. He shrugged and gestured to his chair. What the hell did Laurel think he was going to be able to do should Cam lunge for her?

His vivid imagination pictured blood splashed on the dove gray walls, and despite his better judgment, he pushed himself in between the two combatants. For a tense minute or two, he feared Cam would climb over him to get to her target, but then she sighed, and her mother made a quick about-face.

"Don't bother to show me out," she announced as if she was the one holding the reins of power in the room. "I'm leaving. I'll expect someone to contact me with the details of the memorial service when they're confirmed." She jabbed the button to open the elevator doors and slipped inside, her perfectly made-up face a mask of fury.

The doors slid closed, and Jordan breathed a heavy whoosh of relief.

Cam's posture relaxed, and her hands eased at her sides. "I'm sorry you had to see that."

"To be honest, I'm glad I did," he replied with a smirk. "Bertie would be proud of you."

"Ya think?"

He reconsidered. Bertie, the peacemaker, would've preached for continued patience and understanding. Jordan, on the other hand didn't know how Cam had put up with the abuse for nearly four decades. "Maybe not. But *I'm* proud of you."

"Yeah. Thanks. Great." The words came out in a flat monotone. She collapsed onto the sofa in a heap of mournful fury.

He took her hand and squeezed. "It's gonna be okay, Cam. I promise you."

The first tear escaped, a shimmer of silver that landed on the edge of her inner cheek and stayed there, as if afraid to roll any farther. Cam looked at the empty cushion beside her, then at him in his wheelchair, and back again. "Can you... I mean, is there a way... are you able to...?"

He understood what she had difficulty saying, and with a nod, he held up a hand. Once he maneuvered the chair to a better angle, he used his upper body strength to push himself up, swivel around, and land almost exactly where she'd indicated, give or take a couple of inches.

Her jaw dropped, and her eyes rounded. "Wow."

He settled against the plush sofa back. "Just because I'm in a chair doesn't mean I'm helpless."

"No... I mean, sure... that is, I get it. It's just... it's amazing to see you in action like that. I mean, you were always a great athlete, so it shouldn't come as a surprise, but I guess I never realized..." Her cheeks turned pink, and she stared down at her lap.

He took her hand again, gave another encouraging squeeze to her fingers. "Thanks. It took a lot of hard work and a great rehab specialist. I don't know if I'd be in this good a shape, if not for Marcus."

"Marcus? The man that showed up in Brady's a few weeks ago? He's your rehab specialist?"

"He was. Now, he's my business partner." He reconsidered. "As well as my sports therapist. Best in the country, if you ask me."

Her brow crinkled. "I thought you worked in corporate real estate at HRR."

"I do. But I also want to open a physical therapy and rehab center that will focus on professionals in the tristate area. Athletes, stage performers, that kinda stuff. People who need more intensive training because they put their bodies through more intense workouts as part of their careers. Like I said, Marcus is the best at getting someone into incredible shape. I'm living proof. So, I took the job at HRR, not only for the career change, but also to get a jump on any commercial buildings that might suit our needs to launch our first center." He craned his neck to look directly at her, ready to fill in the gaps she didn't already know. "Originally, I thought the Loughlin site was perfect for our venture."

"What?!" She scrambled against the arm of the sofa, attempting to get to her feet, but he held onto her hand.

"Relax, Cam. I'm not interested in your building. The minute I saw you in it, I realized it belonged to you." She settled down again, but her gaze remained hard, flinty, mentally burrowing into his head as if trying to pull information from his brain through sight alone. "What?"

"You've changed," she murmured, shaking her head. "You're... different. I can't explain it."

He laughed. "*I* can. I got the shit kicked out of me and found out I'm not destined to be the superstar I planned to become. It was a helluva wake-up call. Finding yourself lying helpless in a hospital bed unable to take care of your most basic needs and having to learn how to do stuff that used to come to you naturally is a humbling experience. It certainly knocked me off that pedestal I used to try to balance on."

Her focus returned to her lap. "I'm sorry."

Was she apologizing for abandoning him? He wasn't sure. That was the thing about Cam. Apologies didn't spring from her lips easily. So when she did say those two little words, she rarely elaborated beyond them. For her, it was a blanket statement, meant to cover any misconceptions or hurt feelings she might have inadvertently created. Not because of her ego. Quite the opposite. Cam's self-esteem had been so battered by living with her mother all those years, she never considered anyone put that much weight behind her words or actions.

"It's okay," he assured her.

She dropped her head to his shoulder and wrapped one arm around his waist, a loose hold that might as well have been a vise. He didn't want to move, didn't want time to pass. He'd sit this way forever, if she asked. Nothing else ever seemed so right, so natural. He ran a hand over her hair, reveled in the feel of her in his arms again. Using the pad of his thumb, he brushed away that lone tear.

She sat up and rearranged herself until their lips were a breath apart. "I'm sorry," she said again, and her mouth met his.

She tasted, as she always did, of everything he believed good in the world: sunshine and warm summer grass and freshly fallen snow. Her lips parted beneath his, and his tongue swept inside, needing more of her, burning with a longing to consume all of her, to keep her, to retrieve the woman he'd once loved and lost. He cupped her face between his palms, his fingers pressing gentle circles to her temples, and was rewarded with a low moan that zinged straight through him.

And while a tiny voice tried to warn him that she was still the same woman who'd turned her back on him, his desire for her easily drowned out any misgivings. He loved her, God help him. He always would.

Chapter 13

Albert "Bertie" Wallace was laid to rest with great fanfare on a cloudy, chilly September afternoon. In keeping with the requests made in his will, his memorial service was held in the place he loved most: Vanguard Stadium. A dais was set up on the fifty-yard line, with seats for the friends and family members he'd asked to speak at the event.

All of New York's sports royalty attended, along with the biggest names in city and state politics, local celebrities, and news crews from every network. As a former player-turned-head-coach of the Vanguard, Bertie had impacted a lot of lives over the years. At the end of the speeches, all the guests were invited to pay their respects to Bertie's former wife and beloved stepdaughter. For what seemed like hours, Cam stood next to her mother, neither speaking a word to the other as they accepted condolences from the multitudes of mourners. Since they were not part of Bertie's immediate family, past or present, Mr. Ellison and Jordan remained in the background—nearby if needed, but out of sight. Jordan, however, would never be out of mind. He'd spent the other night on her sofa—but then, so had she.

She didn't really recall how it all happened. There'd been dinner, that confrontation with her mother, and then a conversation that had surprised her for so many reasons. The Jordan she used to know was a good man, but this new Jordan was a better one. He seemed to have more empathy, more generosity to his spirit, and packed a kiss that curled her toes and left her breathless. She stole a glance behind her to watch him and found him watching her. As a blush heated her cheeks, she returned her attention to the people waiting to pay their respects.

Despite her flat shoes, or maybe because of them, her feet ached. Faces and murmured messages of sympathy blurred into a collage of colorful buzz words.

So sorry for your loss...

He's in a better place...

He'll be sorely missed...

Her reaction to the wall of sorrow became robotic: a firm handshake, a whispered thank you, a curt nod, then move along to the next person. That all changed when Paris Redmond reached out to clasp Cam's hand.

"I'm so sorry, Cameron. Bertie was a giant in the sports world. We're all devastated that he's gone."

Cam stiffened, but manners and respect for Bertie would not permit a scene—not here, not now. "Thank you, Paris. Thanks for coming today. It's good to see you again."

Paris should have moved on at that point and allowed the next person in line to pay their respects, but she remained on the platform in front of Cam. "Yes, it's been years, hasn't it? When was the last time? The Aquila Bowl, wasn't it?"

"That was the last time we talked, but, of course, we did see each other in passing at the hospital in Houston."

Paris waved a hand, sending her signature multitude of bangles tinkling in the air. "Ah, yes, that's right. Well, I'm sorry about the circumstances that brought us together again today."

"Thank you." To her relief, Paris finally moved down the line to offer her regards to Laurel, and Cam relaxed.

But before the next person could approach to offer their solemnities, Jordan rolled up beside her. "Did you just tell her you saw her at the hospital in Houston?" At Cam's curt nod, he demanded, "When were you in Houston?"

All she could do was blink at him. "Huh?"

Jordan repeated the question in bullet points. "When... were... you... in... Houston? When did you run into Paris there?"

"At the hospital. The day after your—" She stopped, swallowed. Even now, she couldn't bring herself to mention the injury. "After that game."

"Bull."

"No bull."

He arched a brow at her. "If that's true, why didn't *I* see you there?"

Really? He wanted to have this discussion *now*? Fine. Let's go. She folded her arms over her chest, poised to do battle.

"My guess would be, because you put me on your stupid list. If you'd granted me a modicum of decency, you would have realized I would charter the team jet to get me to you. And that's exactly what I did—about forty minutes after they carried you off the field. I saw the hit. I knew it was bad. I would've gone straight from the tarmac to the ER, if I'd thought I could've been by your side during the surgery. Instead, I spent the night at the hotel across the street and got to the lobby five minutes before visiting hours began the next morning. I wanted to be the first face you saw when you woke up. But apparently, you made sure you didn't have to see me at all. And maybe you were right. Maybe I had no business showing up after what happened between us. But I was terrified for you. Because whether you believe me or not, I still love you. You, obviously, feel differently. I knew you were angry at the way things ended, but I had no idea you hated me so much."

His expression turned stricken. "What the hell are you talking about? I don't hate you. I never hated you."

Hurt and anger whipped her grief into a froth, and her voice rose in volume. "No? You could've fooled me. I mean it would've been one thing if I'd gone to the hospital, security called your room, and you told them you didn't want me to come up. I might have been able to forgive that. But you put me *on a list.* As if you knew I'd show up and you were going to make damn sure I never got close to you. Like I was some... deranged, dangerous stalker. With everything else you were going through, no matter how much pain you were in, within hours of being injured, undergoing surgery and coming out anesthesia, you actually found the time and wherewithal to make sure hospital security had my name at the top of your Do Not Admit list."

"My... 'Do Not...'?" His gaze shot from her to Paris, who had slipped away into the crowd on the other side of the platform. "Son of a—" After giving her hand a quick squeeze, he meandered around where she stood. "We're not done discussing this." Without another word, he motored toward the steel ramp that led down to the field.

"Uh-huh. Sure. Whatever." As Cam watched him speed after Paris, from the corner of her eye, she caught a familiar look of pity on her mother's face, and it froze the blood in her veins. Turning back to the next mourner in line, she told herself she didn't care that Jordan had, once again, publicly ditched her for Paris. To hell with him. And to hell with her mother, too. She'd survive this latest humiliation with her grace and dignity intact. The pain crushing her chest would ease... eventually. Losing Bertie hurt more anyway.

Jordan... well, despite all the changes she'd thought she'd seen in him the other night, Jordan had never really loved her to begin with. Right?

Right.

DAMN, PARIS COULD DASH through a throng—even in her spiky heels. But Jordan wouldn't be deterred from catching up with her. He scanned the crowd for a friendly and useful face and found one. "Luis!" he called out. "Grab Paris."

Luis Blades, retired Vanguard fullback, raced into action. He might have left the gridiron a couple of years ago, but he still had the moves that made him a fan favorite. He faked left, ran right, broke from the people around him. Some of those people, upon seeing the bulk of man in a black suit bearing down on them, scrambled out of the way until, at last, Luis had a straight shot to Paris. As he closed in, with mere feet to go, Luis dove forward, grabbed her by both shoulders the way he would a running back, and held on tight.

Assured she couldn't get away, caged as she was by Luis, Jordan rolled down the ramp and onto the grass. Thank God for the motor on the chair, which made the transition with the briefest chug. When he finally got within earshot of his former agent, he thanked Luis and waited until the fullback had released her arm. "Let's take a walk, Paris. I think we need to have a conversation."

She must have realized he'd trapped her because she stole a quick glance at Luis, who stood by, prepared to pounce again, then flashed Jordan a stunning smile. "Of course. Shall we get a bite to eat? It's bad luck to return straight home from a funeral, you know. There's a charming little bistro on Forty-Sixth. My car is in Lot A."

"What I have to say isn't conducive to a meal." To be honest, depending upon her answers to his questions, he couldn't guarantee he wouldn't cause a scene by lunging for her lying throat. "Let's start by getting away from all these people."

She cast another glance at Luis, and her smile faltered. "All right."

He led the way off the field, past the police officers posted around the entrances and exits, and out of earshot of spectators. He didn't need to make sure she followed; Luis flanked her every step. In fact, he found a bit of humor watching her search beyond him for an exit, then steal a quick glance behind her to see Luis within tackling range.

As Jordan headed for the memorial garden at the side of the stadium, he said nothing, but his insides screamed. When they reached the stone benches in front of the marble effigies of former Vanguard players who'd passed on, a site that would soon include a new member, he gave Luis a curt nod of thanks and sent him back to the memorial service.

"I can handle it from here." He struggled to keep a lid on his percolating emotions until Luis was gone. Then, he went for the jugular. "Tell me how it's possible you saw Cam at the hospital after my injury and not only did I not see her, I never knew she was there."

She took a seat on one of the stone benches and hitched her handbag strap up higher on her shoulder. "Believe me, I was as shocked then as you are now. I mean, it never occurred to me she'd charter a plane and fly halfway across the country to see you—unless she felt the need to gloat."

What was Paris talking about now? "Gloat?"

"Well, why else would she show up? You left *her* team and after two seasons in Texas, wound up sustaining an injury that ended your career. Do you think she came to bring you a fruit basket?"

No. But he didn't, for one second, believe she came to gloat, either. The Cam he knew was a woman of integrity with a heart as deep as the ocean. And like the ocean, she swept away hurt with waves of forgiveness. It took a lot to get her to the stage she reached with her mother the other night. She might have felt betrayed by his sudden departure all those years ago, but it wasn't in her nature to revel in anyone else's pain, not even his.

"Did you happen to ask her why she was there?"

A plane flew overhead, engines screeching, and Paris used the distraction to cross her legs, arranging her skirt to best show off her wasp waist and lean calves.

"I barely saw her," she replied as she opened her handbag and removed a lip balm. "I was racing through the lobby on my way up to see you after your surgery."

"And yet, in all the hours you spent with me after that morning, you never once mentioned she was there."

Paris applied the waxy substance to her lips with deliberate care. "She didn't stick around long enough for me to even think about her. Once she realized she wasn't authorized to get beyond the lobby, she must have turned around and flown home." Paris laughed. "There really isn't more for me to say, except maybe 'I told you so.'"

"You told me so."

After replacing the lip balm and zipping up the purse, she tilted her head toward the sky. "Yes. I told you she would try to keep you tied to her, would hold you back from attaining your full potential just so she'd have a good-looking Vanguard man on her arm for social occasions. Look what she did today, making you escort her to the memorial, allowing the press to assume she had gained the upper hand over you again. You're a nice guy, Jordan, too nice for someone like her. Face it. Like her mother, she eats nice guys as an *amuse bouche*. You should be thanking me for keeping her at bay as long as I did."

"You think so? Were there other times she tried to get to me?"

"Oh, God, probably half a dozen or so. She really thought she had her hooks in you for a while there."

"Like how? When else did you have to run interference for me?"

"Well, let me think. It's been a while. The hospital really was the last time I saw her. Before that, it was just minor stuff. I intercepted birthday cards, and once, she sent a wedding invitation."

"A wedding invitation?"

"Yeah. When her mother married that guy...what was his name?" She snapped her fingers, as if trying to light a spark. "Elton, Elliot..."

"Ellison. Andrew Ellison."

She pointed at him. "That's him. Can you believe it? What was she thinking? That you'd want to be her date?"

Probably. Not that she couldn't have her pick of men, if she asked. Escorting her to public events wasn't about her having a cute guy on her arm, despite what Paris thought. Cam only asked men she trusted implicitly. So few people understood the way Laurel's constant criticism had destroyed Cam's self-esteem over the years. Public events always brought out the worst in Laurel, which brought out Cam's most vulnerable fears. Had he known about the invitation, at the very least, he would've called her to make sure she was okay. Given her a pep talk to get through without him. But, he hadn't even been able to do that much, thanks to Paris.

"So you made sure I didn't see any of this stuff?"

"It's my job to keep my clients focused on the game. If that means I have to remove the little distractions that pop up along the way, I'm not above picking up a thresher." She wriggled her fingers. "I have my spies set up in all aspects of my clients' lives: housekeepers, security personnel, PAs, even a coach or two. It's nothing personal, Jordan. It's good business."

Queasiness washed over him. "You know, Paris, it's too bad you released me from my contract when the surgeons declared my career over. I would have *delighted* in firing your ass right now."

Leaving her sputtering, he headed away from the field where the service continued, away from the memorial garden where, soon, Bertie's likeness would be enshrined.

Jordan had always teased Cam about how much she disliked Paris. Turned out, she was right to be suspicious.

Her words on the dais came back to him. *Because whether you believe me or not, I still love you.*

He was an idiot. Cam might have turned down his marriage proposal, but she'd never stopped loving him. He would need a big play to win her back.

And he'd need it fast.

Chapter 14

She had no idea how she made it to the very last mourner without breaking into tears. Her own fault, really. Because despite the multitude of reasons she had to hate Jordan, she still loved him and always would. What a pathetic loser she was.

She studied the crowd on the dais and the grounds. How many of these people had noticed how quickly he'd abandoned her when Paris popped up? *Paris*, who'd dumped him when an injury ruined his football career, because he was no longer *useful* to her. Maybe that's where she always went wrong. Instead of kicking him to the curb and letting him rot there, she kept welcoming him back into her life. Maybe men were only interested in the women who treated them like garbage.

Okay, fine. She would let him go. This time, for good. She'd survived his departure before. She could do it again. Even if she didn't have Bertie to fall back on this time. Bertie had given her the tools to live her life with passion. Now it was up to her to follow his phenomenal example.

As the crowd began to disperse, she detoured past her mother and Mr. Ellison to exit the makeshift platform.

"Cam?" Mr. Ellison's voice stopped her at the first step.

She turned and waited for him to approach. "Your mother and I are going to Ruby's for lunch. Would you like to join us?"

Cam looked past him to where her mother stood, hands twisting as she watched their interaction while desperately trying to feign indifference.

"For what it's worth," Mr. Ellison whispered, "she's sorry. She knows she went too far last time."

As big a step as Mom had taken in admitting her mistake, Cam shook her head. "I wish I could say that's good enough for me, but she went too far about a thousand miles ago. Maybe someday, we can mend our issues. But for now, I think we're both better off leaving some distance between us. Thanks for the invitation, though."

He offered her a curt nod, his smile nowhere near happy. "I understand. You can divorce a spouse for lots of reasons, but a parent...?" He shrugged.

She took his hand. "You're a nice man. I wish you and my mother years of happiness together."

Before he could say anything else, she descended the stairs and stood on the field. Here was where both her father and Bertie spent so many of their happiest days.

Val appeared at her side. "Hey. You okay?"

She nodded. "I will be, I think. I'll miss him, though."

"Which one? Bertie or Jordan?"

The question jolted her. "Oh, God. You heard that conversation?"

Val wrapped an arm around her shoulder and whispered, "Cam, everyone in the stadium heard you. You were standing right next to a hot mic."

Well, crap. Could this day get any worse? She glanced down at the ground, wishing for a hole to open up and swallow her. But the wish was short-lived.

Straightening her shoulders, she flashed Val a bright smile. "You know what? It's okay. I have nothing to be ashamed of. I'm done playing Little Orphan Cammie for the press and for everyone else." She stole a glance at her mother and Mr. Ellison, making their way off the dais. "I'm a grown-ass woman. I run a multi-million dollar foundation. I'm nobody's victim. It's about time I stopped acting like one. I love Jordan. Turns out, he doesn't love me back. I'm not the first person in New York to suffer from unrequited love; I won't be the last."

Val's eyes widened, but she recovered quickly and gave a curt nod. "Okay, then, grown-ass woman. What happens now?"

"This." On a whim, she took off her shoes and allowed her bare feet to touch the turf all the men she'd loved had once run upon—each at different times.

To her delight, Val followed suit.

"When I was a kid," she told Val, "my dad would bring me here to play two-hand-touch with his teammates' kids. God, it was so much fun!"

The memories evoked all of her senses: the sound of children's laughter, the smell of dirt and grass, the rough texture of the football, the indulgent smiles on the grownups' faces, spicy hot dogs covered in mustard washed down with sugary sodas. Her childhood might have been odd, but at times, it had been a lot of fun.

She took a deep breath in, tilted her face toward the sun, and let the spirit of the men who'd guided her through her formative years fill the empty places in her heart. She'd go on. She had a foundation to run—and a life to live.

"Come on," Val said. "I'll race you to the end zone."

"You're on! Loser buys the first round at Brady's Place. On your mark, get set, go!"

With her flats dangling from her fingertips, she ran forward, the spiky green blades tickling her soles.

Val kept pace, giggling.

From the loudspeaker, the voice of the Vanguard for more than thirty years, Powell Armistead intoned, "Ladies and gentlemen. May I have your attention please?"

She and Val both stopped short, five yards from their goal.

The milling crowd stared upward. It always amused Cam that when an announcer used the sound system in any stadium or theater, everyone would look toward the sky, as if the message came from heaven. "I'd like to direct your attention to the jumbotron on the scoreboard for a special announcement."

What the...?

"Uh-oh," Val said through huffs and puffs. "What's going on now? Did you do this?"

Cam shook her head. Suspicion slinked up her spine. "And it better not be some stunt my mother cooked up, either."

Like the rest of the spectators, she did as Powell directed and stared up at the scoreboard. The photo of Bertie with his name and the year of his birth and death disappeared. The Vanguard logo briefly took its place, then quickly dissolved, and Jordan's face filled the hundred-fifty-foot screen.

"Is that...?" Val stared in wonder, her mouth agape.

Cam was just as speechless. Along with everyone else inside the stadium.

"Did he tape something?"

"I have no idea."

She did note he wore the same suit and tie she'd seen on him since this morning. So, whatever this was, it had to be live—or at the very least, taped today. What the hell was he up to now?

"Hey, folks," he said from the screen. "For those of you who don't know, I'm Jordan Fawcett. A while back, I was a quarterback for the Vanguard. I had a couple of pretty good seasons here, made some great friends, and fell in love with a terrific woman. But I wanted more, more money, more playing time, more of what I thought I deserved. Mostly, I wanted more than what that terrific woman was ready to give me. I was arrogant. And greedy. So when the opportunity arose for me to sign with another team, to have a few more seasons in a place where I could help build a winning enterprise, I took it. I left my teammates, I left my friends, I left the woman I loved."

People stirred around her, staring at her with keen interest. She couldn't move. Her feet had embedded invisible roots in the turf. She could barely draw a breath. All she could do was stare at Jordan's face, her chest tight with dread. What was he doing? And why now, during Bertie's memorial service? *Please, Jordan, please don't break my heart like this. Not today. I'm trying so hard to pick up the pieces. Don't take a sledgehammer to what I've had to rebuild.*

"Cam," Jordan said, and the camera zoomed closer, until all anyone could see on the screen was his face, the intensity of his expression. "You once accused me of leaving you for the first woman who could get me hard."

Around her, murmurs of disgust and discontent rose like a foul wind. Her cheeks blazed, but she kept her head held high, her focus lasered on the screen. She would *not* fall. No matter what he said next, she would *not* fall.

"You were wrong. Lots of women have made me hard since I hit puberty." He flashed a boyish grin. "You're the only woman who ever made me *weak*: weak in the knees every time you're near, weak in the head so I never know if I'm saying something stupid or clever when I try to talk to you. Even now, I'm probably screwing this up. Cam, I love you. I've always loved you. I had no idea you flew to Houston after I was injured. I should've realized you would. It's one of the things I love most about you: your never-ending compassion. If I *had* known, I would've crawled downstairs in my hospital gown, bare-assed and doped-up, just to see you."

Laughter erupted around her, and Cam couldn't bite back a snort of amusement.

"I'm sorry I ever doubted you," he continued, his tone dense with sincerity. "Give me a chance to be the man you need. Let me prove to you we can make it work forever—on our own terms."

Good thing Val was there to catch her by the elbows, to keep her from falling to her knees.

INSIDE THE BROADCAST room, Jordan struggled to figure out what Cam might be thinking about his public apology. What if his declaration of love had come too late? What if she couldn't forgive him?

Well, then, he'd do what he'd just promised in front of a thousand strangers. He'd prove to her they could make their love work forever.

Although he'd managed to get a pretty damn good speech together for the moment, the longer he went without an answer from her, the faster his confidence fled on wings of dread. His tongue grew thick, and his brain misfired. He cleared the block in his throat.

"Cam?" he said into the microphone. "Say something please?"

While his heart thundered in his chest, she strode back to the makeshift dais and, on a screech of feedback, pulled the mic at the podium closer to her mouth. She stared straight up at the windows where he sat. "Are you proud of yourself now?"

"That depends. What did you think?"

"That you used a lot of pretty words I've heard from you before." She folded her arms over her chest. "Go back to Paris. I have nothing more to say, Jordan."

"I was never involved with Paris. Not in a romantic way. Did I listen to Paris? Yes. She was my agent. Did I trust her? God help me, I did. And I realize now I shouldn't have. She filtered my mail, Cam. She screened my visitors in the hospital, and I never knew anything about it 'til now. She told security to keep you from me. So to any of my compatriots out there who still have Paris Redmond representing them, be aware she has spies set up everywhere. And if someone tells you they've been trying to reach you, but you're not getting back to them, believe them. It's Paris who's keeping you isolated." He shook his head. "But this isn't about her. Not when it comes to you and me, Cam. *I* screwed up. I gave her all that power because it was easier than taking responsibility for my life and facing up to what I did to you, to this team, to everybody who cared about me."

"She filtered your mail?" Cam's tone held a scalpel's edge. "Did she tie up your fingers so you couldn't call, either?"

He sighed. She wouldn't make this easy on him. But he'd do whatever it took to make her believe him, to win her back to his side again. "I blamed you. When you turned down my proposal, I thought it was because you didn't care. But that's not why you said no, is it? I get it now. You, of all people, have every right to doubt a marriage leads to happily ever after."

There was a good chance he'd just insulted her mother, but he didn't care. All that mattered was reaching out to Cam and convincing her to give him—give *them*—a second chance.

"I should have never doubted that you love me, that despite not wanting to marry me, you hadn't given up on me, or us. Because when *you* love someone, you love them forever. And I'm sorry. I'm so sorry. All this time, we've wasted. I wish I could take it all back. I wish I'd waited before running off to Houston. But I can't change what's happened before. All I can do is move forward. And I'm asking you to move forward with me. I want to shower you with that same never-doubting, forever kind of love. Give me a chance. Give *us* a chance. Please."

She met his plea with dead silence. Not a sound came from anywhere in the stadium. Time stood still, and he held his breath until his chest ached.

Just when he thought he'd lost, she shouted into the mic. "Well? What are you waiting for? Get down here and kiss me."

His chest expanded, and he gave a whoop, then a thumbs-up to Powell. He leaned into the mic. "I'm a little slow these days. Meet me halfway?"

"I'll race you," she replied. "But don't think I'm giving you a head-start because of that chair."

No. She'd never show him pity. Empathy, yes. Sympathy when warranted. Bucket loads of love, encouragement, kindness, and loyalty. But Cam would make him face his challenges head-on, not avoid them. She was his greatest cheerleader, his strength, and his weakness. He wouldn't have her any other way.

He left the booth and for the millionth time since that damn sack he took in Houston, he cursed his inability to run. Lucky for him, going down the ramps from the broadcast booth was easier than going up had been. The incline wasn't steep, and the multitude of curves kept him from picking up too much speed and careening out of control. Still, he wished he could go faster.

He'd meant it when he told her, if he had to crawl the last few yards to reach her, bare-assed and doped-up, he would. Whatever it took, he'd find his way back to the woman he'd callously left behind. They'd wasted so much time already. Every second that kept them apart now was torturous.

He rounded another turn and suddenly, there she was, barefoot and out of breath. She paused long enough for him to set the brakes on his chair before she ran the last few yards and launched herself into his lap.

He gathered her close to him, reveling in the scent of her, the feel of her, the nearness of her. He cupped her face in his hands. "God, Cam, I can't believe I ever let you go. I'm so sorry. So goddamn sorry."

"Shut up and kiss me, Jordan."

He captured her lips with his, breathed her into his lungs, received her forgiveness and offered his love to her in return.

From outside, a rhythmic applause and chant created a booming song.

Cam broke their kiss to stare at the gate closest to them. "What *is* that?"

He nuzzled her collarbone. "Who cares?"

When she pushed away as if to leave his lap, he wrapped an arm around her waist. "Okay, okay. We'll look."

He released the brake on his chair and headed through the gate. The cement walls echoed the noise, increasing the volume and the thunderous bass of the crowd's clapping. They left the dim tunnel leading to the fold-up seats in this section of the stadium and came outside to the railing where several levels below, people still littered the football field looking up at the various gates and sections, clapping and shouting in unison.

"Cam and Jor-dan!" *Clap, clap, clap.* "Cam and Jor-dan!" *Clap, clap, clap.*

Jordan recognized Cam's assistant, Val, leading the chant from the dais's microphone. While he watched, Val's attention swerved, and she pointed to the scoreboard. The crowd's chanting quickly became a wave of cheers and mad applause. Because there, up on the jumbotron screen, was the image of Cam snuggled up against him as they looked down upon the melee on the field.

As if on cue, the clouds parted, and a strong single beam of sunlight fell on them. Heat warmed his face, and he stared up at the brightened sky.

"I'm guessing that's Bertie's way of saying he's pretty happy with us right now."

"So am I," she replied and kissed him again.

Chapter 15

Cam stood behind Jordan as he and Marcus each took hold of the giant scissors and cut the tape on their professional sports therapy center. A light smatter of applause greeted their efforts from the small crowd of supporters surrounding them.

"Welcome," Marcus announced as he pushed the button to open the wide, glass double-doors. "Come on in!"

Cam allowed Jordan the honor of entering on his own and turned to speak with Marcus's wife, Theresa. "It looks great, doesn't it?"

"It's amazing," the other woman enthused. "I'm so proud of them!"

Cam laughed. "There were times I wasn't sure they'd ever stop arguing over what went where."

Theresa poked an elbow in Cam's side. "You got *that* right."

On the inside, the space had been perfectly apportioned for equipment, exercise areas, a sauna, and a holistic center complete with massage tables and an acupuncture office. They'd even installed a lap pool and a jetted tub for hydrotherapy patients.

Once all the guests entered, Theresa joined her husband near the office area where a table had been set up with non-alcoholic drinks and appetizers. Other members of the therapy staff, wearing black t-shirts emblazoned with the center's turquoise and white logo, milled around the equipment, showing guests how each piece worked, what muscle groups would be affected and how.

Cam returned to Jordan's side. She placed a hand on his shoulder and gave an encouraging squeeze. "Congratulations. It's perfect."

"Yeah. I can't believe it's finally done and ready." He settled his hand on top of hers, then lifted both hands to place a kiss inside her palm.

She instinctively curled her fingers closed, like a child clutching a perfect pebble within her grasp. These days, every kiss, every tender moment was precious. Life was a treasure chest, and love was the jewel inside. Without the jewel, the chest was just a box, like any other box. It might be fancier or made from better components, depending upon a person's circumstances, but it was still an empty box. On the other hand, fill the box with love, the true jewels of life, and the box's worth increased exponentially.

"Outstanding, Jordan." Susan Harwich approached them, hand outstretched to shake Jordan's. "The place looks incredible. I always knew you had a real talent for this line of work. You can spot the diamonds in a coal mine. That's a gift." She quirked a brow, but humor rode high in the sparkle in her eyes. "You sure I can't coax you back to HRR?"

"I'm sure. I appreciate all you did for me, Susan. You gave me a chance when I was getting my life back together, and you got Marcus and me a great deal on this property—"

"I got you a *killer* deal." Her toothy smile resembled a shark's, and Cam suppressed a shiver. "And I got a little revenge while I was at it. Bella will think twice before encroaching on my territory again. All in all, this was one of my best deals ever. Thanks to you."

He shook his head. "Unh-uh. This was all your doing. Between the price you negotiated and your construction contacts coming through for us, we came in far enough under budget to install all Marcus's dream equipment. Which went a long way to putting him at ease after I let you take your time getting us all to the table. You've made me look like a hero. So, thank *you*. And I'm also grateful that you put me in touch with your clients on the Island. They've been a big help in getting my new realty office launched."

Cam took a step back, allowing the two business associates to have a private discussion about corporate properties and slaying your dragons, whatever that meant.

While Jordan was a partner in this new therapy venture, he preferred to be the silent kind while he continued pursuing commercial real estate for fun and profit, working closer to their new home.

"Cameron?"

At the sound of her mother's hesitant voice, she turned to find the woman striding forward, hands clasped at waist-height in front of her and twisting with nervousness. Mr. Ellison stood at Mom's side, his arm draped around her shoulders in a protective stance.

Guilt pierced Cam at the sight. Her mother was afraid of her. Not of any physical harm, but of what Cam might *say* to hurt her.

She'd done that, caused those haunted eyes and deep lines around Mom's mouth. The two of them had always shared a contentious connection. But no incident was as contentious as their argument the night Bertie died. That night was the first time she'd ever thrown her mother out of her apartment or refused to apologize after her temper cooled. And she'd kept her mother at arms' length ever since.

Love, she reminded herself. *The treasure is love. Without love, the chest is empty.*

She might have a twisted way of showing it at times, but her mother loved her. And after all this time apart, maybe today was the day to begin mending their torn relationship. Like a grown-ass woman who had a lot of love to give would do.

"Hello, Mother. I'm so glad you could come." She bent to give Mom a quick air kiss, careful not to smear the perfect makeup or wrinkle the silk blouse.

Jordan cleared his throat. "Susan, why don't I show you around the site?"

"No, Jordan, wait." Mom laid a hand on the back of his chair. "Please?" When he paused, she pointed at him, then Cam. "I need to speak with you both. I promise I won't take up more than a minute of your time. You two. You're happy?"

Cam and Jordan joined hands again. "Yes," Cam replied. "Blissfully so."

Mom nodded. "Good. That's good. And the new school? It's working out for the foundation?"

"Yes. Faculty and kids are all delighted." Cam felt Jordan apply a light pressure to her fingers, a prompt to move forward from their animosity. He'd been the one to invite her mother to the opening today, insisting it was long past time for the two women to bury the hatchet. "You... umm... you and Mr. Ellison haven't been to our new place yet. Maybe you'd like to join us for dinner next Saturday? If you're available?"

Her mother beamed and shared a joyful glance with her husband, who nodded. "That would be wonderful."

"We live out in the 'burbs now, Mother," Cam teased. "You know that, right?"

"Yes. The birthday card you sent this year had your new address on it. I'm looking forward to seeing the house."

"It's beautiful," she replied. "A sprawling ranch on an acre of wooded property in a great neighborhood with lots of shops and galleries in town. It's perfect for us. No need for Jordan to worry about elevators and staircases. His office is a five-minute drive from the house. We even got a dog! An Australian shepherd we named Hudson. He's big and goofy, and he's got plenty of space to run around the grounds. Or we can take him through the wildlife preserve down the road with its wide paths and walking trails. Some days, if you're there at the right time, you can see deer. It's an entirely different way of life: slower, quieter, and infinitely more relaxing. Wait 'til you see it. You might like it so much you decide to move there yourself."

Mom gave a delicate shiver. "Don't be ridiculous, Cameron. Why would I ever leave the city for the sticks?"

"Ahem!" Mr. Ellison's not-so-subtle interjection caused her mother to duck her head.

"I'm sorry. I didn't mean to suggest—that is, I'm sure it's lovely, and I can't wait to see it. But you know I'm a creature of habit, a metropolitan denizen from the day I was born. I have my routines and my showroom and my vendors. Everything I know is here. If I want quiet, I take a few days out at the summer cottage in the Hamptons. I don't think I could ever live like that full-time, though. You and I are very different that way. You're far braver than I am. And a lot more flexible when life throws you a curve."

Wow. Cam had never seen her mother back down so quickly. And with such graciousness. Maybe Mr. Ellison would finally be the husband Mom needed, the man who took control and kept it, pushing her out of her comfort zone and keeping her on her toes. She hoped so. She really did want her mother to be happy—and settled.

She let loose a laugh, subtle but joyful. "You're probably right. I'm still anxious for you to see the place, though. And should you decide you need quiet in the future, you could come and visit. You'd be more than welcome. We've got plenty of space. And we could have a few mother-daughter outings in the area. I've been ceding more and more of the day-to-day operations of the New York office to Val. She's a godsend, I swear. The foundation's in very good hands with her. I'm actually considering opening a satellite office out by us, a new project for me to focus on. You know how hard it is for me to sit still. Of course, that'll only happen if Jordan can find us the perfect location again, the way he did with the Loughlin building."

"So everything's worked out for you." Her mother waited for Cam to nod, then turned her attention to Mr. Ellison. "There. See? I told you it would be all right."

"Tell them, sweetheart." Mr. Ellison's tone, while soft and sweet, was laced with steel.

Uh-oh. Cam stiffened, braced for some horrible news. Tell them what?

Her mother planted her hands on her hips. "I don't see why it's such a big deal. I was right, wasn't I?"

Cam's nerves skittered and popped. *Oh, Mother, what did you do?*

"Tell them," Mr. Ellison repeated. "Go on. They have a right to know."

Know what? Whatever it was, Cam wasn't so sure she had the right or the desire to know. She gripped Jordan's hand, nearly crushing his bones as dread tightened her every nerve ending.

"It's about the Loughlin building," her mother said with a defeated sigh. "Technically, Jordan didn't find the place. I used my influence on the board to insist we only sell the site to the Delgado Foundation and that Jordan Fawcett was to be the agent of record on the deal."

"So *you* were the anonymous board member!" Susan Harwich exclaimed with a finger of accusation. "Of course. It all makes sense now."

Her mother nodded, but she kept her focus pinned to Cam. "I knew it was perfect for your needs, and I knew that if I brought it to your attention, you'd be against even looking at the place simply because I was the one to suggest it. You would've remained too stubborn to see the potential."

Cam would've liked to argue, but how could she? Her mother was, sad to say, one hundred percent right. She would never have considered a site her mother pushed, always looking for the ulterior motive behind the offer.

Luckily, her mother didn't wait for an agreement or a denial.

"All I've ever wanted," Mom continued, "was for you to be happy. And you are, aren't you? I did the right thing, didn't I? Cam, I waited years for you to bounce back from what happened between you and Jordan. When you didn't, and it seemed like you weren't ever going to look for love again, I assumed you two might have unfinished business between you. I did some research. Found out that, like you, Jordan had never married, wasn't dating, and I was thinking, maybe you two needed a push. Then I learned he had actually returned to New York and I knew what I had to do." She shrugged. "It seemed like fate to me. So obvious any idiot would see it. And now you two are together and you're happy, right?"

"I *was*," Cam said. "But now that I know you manipulated us both..." She shook her head.

The hurt on her mother's face stuck a knife in her heart. And she reconsidered what she planned to say.

The treasure is love. Her mother loved her. So, okay, in her twisted way, she'd set them up, in order to bring them back together. But after that initial bit of meddling, she'd left them both to their own devices to sink or swim. In the end, they had created their own happily ever after. All Mom had done was push. They'd done the hard work on their own.

Cam hardened her expression to stone and kept her tone harsh. "Well, then, I guess there's only one thing left to say." She pulled her mother into a tight hug and crooned in her ear, "Thank you."

Her mother stiffened in her arms. "You're not angry?"

She pulled away, laughing. "You gave me the best gift ever. A second chance with the man I love. How could I possibly be angry with that?"

"Well, if learning about your mother's interference has put you in such a good mood..." Jordan interjected, "this might be the right time for a fumblerooski." He turned his chair so that he directly faced Cam. The others around them all took a step back, and several more guests joined the circle, including Theresa and Marcus, as if they all anticipated some grand event would take place that they'd be witness to.

A befuddled Cam, when asked later, would admit she never recognized the signs. Until Jordan reached into his pocket and took out a small, blue jewelry box she'd seen once before, several years ago. Too much had happened in the last few minutes for her brain to fully comprehend the gravity of the moment.

"Cam, I love you. I've always loved you. I'll go to my grave loving you. But until then, I want to spend every breath we have together with you. On *your* terms, whatever they may be." He flipped open the lid to reveal the square-cut diamond glittering on its bed of sapphire velvet. "So, I'm giving you this ring, as a symbol of all I feel for you. The choice is yours what to do with it. Place it on your right hand and we'll go on at your pace until you feel comfortable with my promise of forever. When you're ready to talk about an engagement, maybe a wedding sometime far in the future, you can move it to your left hand. Or, you can just keep it in the box for the rest of our lives. The choice is entirely up to you. What do you say?"

She was ready. She was more than ready. Eagerly, she pulled the ring from the box and slid it onto the finger of her left hand. "I love you too, Jordan. And I want to spend every breath I have left by your side. The wedding can wait, but for now, I'm happy to be engaged."

While everyone broke into spontaneous applause and cheers, he pulled her onto his lap. She roped her left arm around his neck, extending her hand to admire the glint of the diamond beneath the overhead lights.

Nuzzling his collarbone, she whispered, "I can't believe you kept this ring all these years."

He chuckled and murmured in her ear. "I kept the suit, too. I thought it might be unlucky to wear it again today, but you gotta have hope, right?"

Hope. Sure, you had to have hope. But more importantly, you had to have love. She gazed at the happiness streaming to them from the people they'd touched, the people who cared, and her focus landed once again on first her mother, and then Jordan.

"Hope and a treasure chest full of love." She placed her lips on his and allowed love to carry them both forward to their future.

BOOKS BY GINA ARDITO
THE MONEY SERIES
The Bonds of Matri-money
A Run for the Money

That's Amore!

THE NOBODY SERIES
Nobody's Darling
Nobody's Business
Nobody's Perfect

Chasing Adonis
Duping Cupid

THE AFTERLIFE SERIES
Eternally Yours
In Your Dreams
Waiting in the Wings

THE CALENDAR GIRLS SERIES
Charming for Mother's Day
Duet in September
Reunion in October

Homecoming in November
Memories in December

Even Now
A Love to Keep Me Warm
Lightning in a Bottle
Echoes of Love

ANTHOLOGIES
Kaleidoscope Hearts 2

DEAR READER,

Thanks so much for reading PLAY ACTION PASS. I started writing this story about fifteen years ago when my son was playing in his local Peewee football league. I was Team Mom with all the responsibilities that entailed: snacks; coordinating parent volunteer services; staying on the field in driving rain, muggy mosquito-filled nights, and blustery fall evenings. I always brought my Alphasmart to write on, and the other parents would tease me about the possibility I'd one day use my experiences on the field to write a football romance.

I wrote the first two chapters of this story during that time, then stalled. And there Cam and Jordan sat, in my "Unfinished drafts" folder on my computer. Until last year.

Fast forward fifteen years, my football-playing child is now in law school, and I needed a quick story I could pull up and finish for an anthology with eight other authors. PLAY ACTION PASS found a home within the pages of KALEIDOSCOPE HEARTS 2. But in order to make it fit the format the anthology required, a lot of scenes and conflicts wound up on the proverbial cutting room floor.

Thus, when the anthology was removed from sale and I reacquired the rights to my characters and their romance, I taped together all the bits and pieces I'd had to cut from the first edition. I loved writing this story the way I'd always envisioned it, and I hope you enjoyed reading this version.

If you did enjoy it, I'd like to ask a favor. Please consider writing a review on your favorite retail site? Amazon, BookBub, Goodreads, or just recommend it on Facebook to your friends and family members! Independent authors such as myself need those reviews in order to compete with bigger names and bigger houses with bigger budgets for advertising. Like other small businesses, I rely on word of mouth to find new readers. Your voice helps. And yes, I do read my reviews. Good or bad, I appreciate whenever a reader takes the time to share their thoughts about my work.

You can contact me at gina@ginaardito.com or through my website, https://ginaardito.com.

Want to be among the first to know about new books and have input into story lines and cover art? Sign up for my monthly newsletter[1]! You can also follow me on BookBub[2], Facebook[3], Twitter[4], and Instagram[5].

---

1.   *https://landing.mailerlite.com/webforms/landing/w7a0f0*

2.   *https://www.bookbub.com/authors/gina-ardito*

3.   *https://www.facebook.com/GinaArditoAuthor/*

And of course, be sure to check out my backlist for other stories that will make you fall in love...with your laugh!

Until next time, stay safe, share love, and be well!

Fondly,
Gina

---

4.   *https://twitter.com/GinaArdito*

5.   *https://www.instagram.com/ginaardito/*

About the Author

Gina Ardito is the award-winning author of more than twenty-five romances in contemporary, historical, and paranormal sub-genres. In 2012, she launched her freelance editing business, Excellence in Editing, and now has a stable of award-winning clients, as well.

She's hosted workshops around the world for writing conferences, author organization chapter meetings, and library events. To her everlasting shame, despite all her accomplishments, she'll never be more famous than her dog, who starred in commercials for 2015's Puppy Bowl.

Read more at https://ginaardito.com/.

www.ingramcontent.com/pod-product-compliance
Lightning Source LLC
Chambersburg PA
CBHW052004220626
47052CB00004B/1084